THE
GIRLS
OF
GETTYSBURG

BOBBI
MILLER

Holiday House / New York

Library of Congress Cataloging-in-Publication Data

Miller, Bobbi.
Girls of Gettysburg / by Bobbi Miller. — First edition.
pages cm
Summary: "Pickett's Charge, one of the bloodiest battles of the Civil War,
is the climax of this Civil War adventure, told from the perspective of three girls:
a Union loyalist, a free Black, and a girl from Virginia who disguised herself
as a boy to fight in the Confederate Army"—Provided by publisher.
Includes bibliographical references.
ISBN 978-0-8234-3163-2 (hardcover : alk. paper)
[1. Gettysburg, Battle of, Gettysburg, Pa., 1863—Fiction.
2. United States—History—Civil War, 1861–1865—Participation, Female—Fiction.
3. Sex role—Fiction.]   I. Title.
PZ7.M61234Gi 2014
[Fic]—dc23
2013045645

For Karen, who believed in my dreams.

The future belongs to those who believe
in the beauty of their dreams.
                                    Eleanor Roosevelt

On July 3, 1863, twelve thousand Confederate soldiers stood on Seminary Ridge, to the west of Gettysburg, Pennsylvania, armed and ready to join the fight. Almost a mile away, at the end of an open field, a copse of trees marked the Union line standing firm on Cemetery Ridge. When the signal was given, the men marched across the field. The line had advanced less than two hundred yards when the Federals sent shell after shell howling into their midst.

Boom! Boom! Boom! Shells pummeled the marching men. As one man fell in the front of the line, another stepped up to take his place. Smoke billowed into a curtain of white, thick and heavy as fog, stalking them.

Still they marched on.

Boom! Men fell legless, headless, armless, black with burns and red with blood. Still they marched on across that field.

When the smoke cleared, more than six thousand men lay dead or dying on the field. For days after the battle, the townspeople of Gettysburg buried the dead and tended the wounded. One Union soldier on burial detail came upon a shocking find: the body of a female Confederate soldier. But everyone knew girls were not strong enough to do any soldiering; they were too weak, too pure, too pious to be around roughhousing boys. That was why girls were not allowed to enlist in the army. So how could this ragtag girl be in the middle of a bloody battlefield? She carried no papers, so he could not identify her; instead, he buried her in an unmarked grave. A Union general noted her presence at the bottom of his report. His words—"one female (private) in rebel uniform"—became her epitaph. Her story remains a mystery.

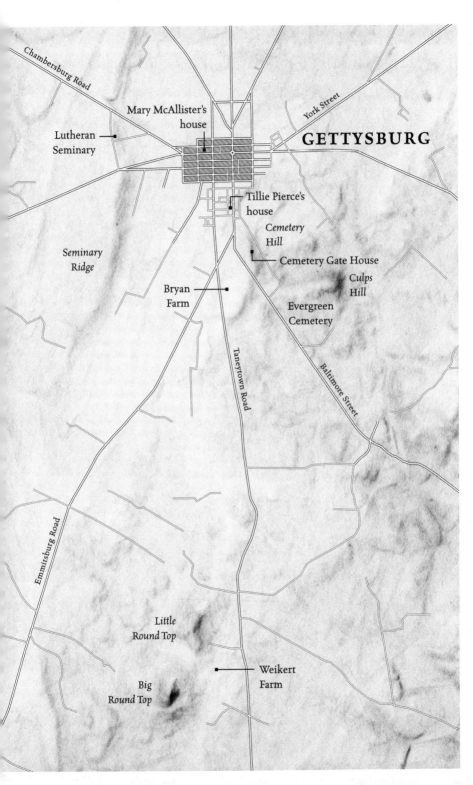

PART ONE

NORTH . . .

May 1863

CHAPTER ONE

ANNIE

Annie sank lower in the water, like a frog in her swamp. She hid in the thick of water lilies and huckleberry overhang, moving so slow the water forgot to ripple in her wake. The morning air was thick with heat and haze, thick as grits. She couldn't see the Yanks. But she could hear their boots scraping against dirt and stone, and their voices raised in anger, looking for something.

Or someone.

They were like flies swarming in a pigsty, those Yanks, tramping along the muddy path.

One loomed out of the haze as he swerved off the path, easing near the water's edge. He stood so close she could hear his ragged breathing. Blood stained his coat and britches. His face, too, was smeared with blood, but she couldn't tell if it was his. His rifle raised, he scanned the water with hooded eyes.

Annie fingered the trigger on her rifle-musket. She couldn't shoot, not this close, or more Yanks might pounce on her like buzzards drawn to fresh kill. Her eyes flicked to the woods behind him, up the path and then down, seeing how close they might be. Suddenly the Yank froze, lowering his rifle directly at her.

"I see you, boy, there in the shadow," he growled. "Show yourself."

She heard the click as he pulled the hammer back.

Annie stood up from her crouch, pulling the brim of her hat low on her brow, and stepped out of the shadow. The Yank's eyes narrowed, taking in the full measure of her. He was as ragged as her sister's

3

corn-husk doll, his cheeks hollowed from hunger, his hair greasy and straggly. His bloodstained shirt seemed too big for his scarecrow arms.

This Yank was too hunger-dizzy to see through her disguise.

His finger trembled as his red-rimmed eyes fell on her musket. "That's a mighty fine gun, boy. How did a ragged puke such as you come into possession of such a rarefied find?"

Annie said nothing, tightening her grip on the gun.

"You gonna shoot me, boy?" The Yank smiled, his teeth brown with rot.

"I ain't giving you my gun." She lowered her voice to gravel, digging her heels into the mud.

The Yank chuckled. "Boy, I will shoot if'n you don't give me that gun."

Annie inhaled deep, shaking her head slowly.

The Yank grinned at her. And then a shot rang out.

I'm done for, for sure! Annie winced.

But the Yank let loose a gurgling cry as his eyes rolled white, and he slumped forward into the mud.

Annie didn't wait around to see who it was that shot, rebel or Yank. She shot off like a bullet herself. Holding her musket over her head, she slogged through the swampy water, not looking back. Half-crawling, half-dashing through the brambles, she trudged toward the shore, where finally she made it into the woods and disappeared into the shadows.

Like her brother always told her, you've got to charge ahead sometimes, come what may, through hell and high water. Just keep moving till you get where you're going. And she was going north, to join the army, where she'd find herself plenty of Yanks to kill.

CHAPTER TWO

GRACE

Grace coughed.

The day was butter-melting hot. And the classroom, set in the back of the windowless church, was so stifling, it snatched the very air out of her. The back door was opened in hopes of moving fresh air into the room, but the breeze only stirred up the dust.

Grace was worried about Millie. Millie hadn't come to school this morning, and she feared the worst. Rumors flew persistent as mosquitoes on hot, swampy days: *The rebels are coming.* She overheard Mamma telling Pappa how the rebs had been sneaking across the line, stealing into the homes of freemen, arresting entire families as fugitive slaves, taking them back to Richmond. For weeks now, one family after another had packed what they could carry on their backs and left under cover of night. The town was almost deserted of Negroes now.

Every day someone didn't come to class, and everyone knew what that meant—they had fled north.

And today Millie hadn't come.

Millie and Grace were best friends. They were going to become teachers together. Millie wouldn't leave, not without saying good-bye. Not unless something terrible had happened.

Pappa wasn't leaving. He had a farm to work. Despite all the rumors, he didn't believe the rebs would dare cross the river. Pappa was proud as a mountain, and there was no moving him if he didn't want to be moved. Not even that General Lee could move Pappa.

"I was born a free man, as was my mamma and pappa," he often reminded Mamma. "This is my home, our home, *here in Gettysburg*. I will *not* be moved from my home."

"Stubborn old man," Mamma barked. Unlike Pappa, Mamma was always afraid. Living so close to the Mason-Dixon Line did that to her. She wanted to leave, run as fast as she could and head north. It was like a nervous tic, her fear.

"What is it that we can do here? Are you allowed to carry a gun to protect yourself? You sell the finest wheat and fruit to them, but are you allowed to shop in their stores? You pay taxes, but can you vote? Grace has the brightest mind of any child I've ever seen, and is she allowed to go to the Young Ladies' Seminary?"

"You'll see, someday Grace *will* teach at a fine school. You'll see, my baby girl will find her way when this war ends. Mr. Lincoln—and I—will see to that!"

"You think too highly of this president, Abraham Bryan. His own people hate him. They even tried to kill him, and they'll succeed one day, you mark my words. This president may find a way to end *this* war," Mamma had said. "But the bigger war will never end."

Grace turned, watching Mamma as she stood at the head of the class. Mamma loved teaching, but she didn't like coming to school these days. It was just a short trip from the farm to this church, no more than a half-hour walk through the orchard and past the fields. But it scared Mamma to be in the open.

Mamma smoothed her bun as she read, stumbling through the words. Then she looked up and sent Grace one of her Be Still looks. Grace smiled back, willing her foot to stop tap-tapping.

But it didn't stop. *Tap-tap-tap.*

"Well." Mamma closed the reader. "I can see we'll not accomplish anything more today!" She dismissed the class with a wave of her hand. "Go home straightaway, now! No dawdling, do you hear me?"

Grace made a mad dash to the door. "I have to check on Millie!"

Grace walked, then ran, along Taneytown Road into Gettysburg. Other children skittered around her, shouting and dancing down the road.

Suddenly a voice hailed her.

"Grace Bryan, stop there!"

Grace turned on her heel to face Tillie Pierce. Only a handful of years older than herself, and a hand taller, Tillie sure thought of herself as older and taller. She was the butcher's daughter, and a student at the Young Ladies' Seminary.

"Should you be here?" asked Tillie.

"Why not?" Grace asked.

"Why, with the war almost here in Gettysburg, just beyond the river, and so many of your kind leaving as fast as they might, I just thought your father would have taken you north by now."

Grace could see that Tillie was trying to smile; maybe she was even trying to be nice. But unlike her fancy dress with the lace trim, it just didn't fit very well. And then she noticed that Tillie was hiding something in her apron. She didn't fool Grace: Tillie Pierce had stolen some of Pappa's peaches.

"Pappa isn't going anywhere." Grace smiled in return, a wide smile. "No one chases us off our land—not rebels, not anyone. But here I was thinking your father had left, too. I am glad to see we are both wrong."

"What do you mean?" Tillie lost her smile and stiffened. "Why would my father leave?'

"With so many of your kind fleeing north, I just thought your father had taken you as well."

"My *kind*?" Tillie was squaring her shoulders. "What on earth are you prattling on about?"

"You know, *your* kind . . . Republicans." Grace dashed off down the road, not wanting to listen to any more from Tillie Pierce. Tillie didn't mean to be rude; she just didn't know any better.

In the south part of town, she ran past a neat row of white board houses, each surrounded by a small rail fence, chickens pecking in the yards. Near the end of the road was Millie's house. It was dark inside. Only the curtains moved in the breeze.

"Millie!" she pushed open the gate.

"I'm sorry, Gracie."

Grace whirled about to face Miss Mary McAllister.

Miss Mary smiled. She was as plump as Pappa was tall, with bright red curls flying in every direction all the way down her back. Miss Mary's store was a couple of blocks down the way, closer to the diamond in the middle of town. If it had been anyone else, Grace would have wondered how they came to be in this row of houses. But Miss Mary was a mountain, just like Pappa, and just like Pappa, she had her own way of doing things.

"They left last night, Grace," said Miss Mary. "Mrs. James was just too afraid to stay. And you shouldn't be here, child. You should be home with your mamma."

"She didn't say good-bye." Grace's stomach pinched.

"Millie will be back, Gracie. She told me to tell you, she'll be back." Miss Mary patted Grace's arm gently.

Grace shook her head in disbelief. Maybe Tillie was right. If Millie had left, then maybe Pappa was going to make her and Mamma leave Gettysburg.

CHAPTER THREE

TILLIE

Her kind, indeed! Tillie huffed, glancing over her shoulder, watching as Grace Bryan disappeared over the rise. So what if she had taken some peaches? With all those trees, surely taking six peaches couldn't matter. But Grace's mother would make a big fuss and tell Mother. And Mother would scold her with heated tongue and pointed finger.

"Proper young ladies do not behave in such a wild manner!" Mother would shrill. "Surely they teach you manners at the Young Ladies' Seminary?"

Mother always said everyone had their proper place in the world, and Tillie should behave in the manner appropriate to her station in life.

Tillie huffed. She didn't take the peaches for herself. Mother was in a constant fret these days about the war. Tillie hoped these would help ease her spirit some. No one would fault her for taking a few peaches.

Tillie walked faster, wrapping the peaches tighter in her lace apron, careful not to bruise them.

Never in all her fourteen years had she seen Gettysburg in such an uproar. In fact, this little town always had an irksome quiet to it. Nothing ever happened here.

Until now. And she found it all so very exciting!

Tillie's brothers belonged to the Pennsylvania Reserves, near enough to come home every few days. They looked so sharp and dignified in their uniforms. And, many a time, they brought handsome comrades home for dinner, and the evenings became fine soirees of poetry and piano and Mother's pies.

Oh! They were so dashing, those soldiers in their uniforms! And they told of the most glorious adventures in faraway places.

Tillie promised herself that one day she'd see some faraway places of her own. She'd go to Philadelphia, to Boston, maybe all the way to San Francisco!

PART TWO

ANNIE

May 1863

CHAPTER FOUR

Not done yet. As far as Annie had come, she still had a ways to go. She couldn't breathe easy, not just yet.

The carriage rumbled along the rutted road. Annie bounced as the wheels hit another deep pit. They had traveled now for more than an hour without saying a word. She was accustomed to the moods of older people, and let the dandified lawyer be in his thoughts. She'd seen it in Pap. Since the war began, Pap had sunk into his own despair, his blue eyes draining of their sky color, even as his mood turned dark and explosive like musket fire.

Her brother William had been the eldest son and Pap's true pride. William was smart enough to go to school, smart enough to be a doctor. He was going to take over the farm and bring the soil back to life. But like all of Virginia's sons, William had volunteered for the army. He had been killed at Manassas.

Her brother James had been the second son, and he was also Annie's twin. So filled with liquid fire to avenge the death of William, he ran off to volunteer. Too young to fight, too stubborn to quit, the officer liked his spunk and made him a drummer.

Annie tightened her grip on her rifle, scanning the woods ahead of them. This rifle-musket she carried now had been a Christmas present for James. It was a rare one—a Whitworth, and not a finer rifle was ever made. Pap had sold his favorite colt to a Georgia cavalry officer in exchange for the Whitworth. He had hung it on the mantel in wait for James to come home.

But James never did come home. He came down with the fever, and died three months after William.

The war spread all across Virginia like a storm surge, leaving in its wake a ravaged land. There had been no one tougher than Mama, and no one bigger than Pap. But the war had crushed them both. Pap died in his heartbreak. Then Mama took herself and the girls to live with Aunt Bess. Aunt Bess had strict ideas about a girl's proper place in society, and she meant to teach Annie how to become a proper lady.

But Annie had different plans.

Mama always warned Annie that she had too much gumption and not enough sense. "Fish don't fly and bees don't swim for a reason," Mama said.

Annie guessed it was true enough that her stubborn nature could put a mule to shame. Mama had told her to pick her battles. "You're always at war with someone. Your brother. Your father. Your Aunt Bess," Mama said. "Just learn your place and quit fighting everything that crosses your path. You'll be a much happier person."

But no one was going to tell Annie her proper place!

So Annie decided to run. The idea came with the boom and flash of a sudden summer storm, the moment she saw the advertisement. It had been posted by a widow, Mrs. Margaret Trudeau of Portsmouth. Mrs. Trudeau needed a substitute to keep her grandson out of the army, and she'd pay three hundred dollars for the right man. Strange how money can reduce a life to the same level as a jar of peaches, all up for bargaining, Annie thought. But three hundred dollars! That was some powerful money that could get her away from all that grief and ruin. And from Aunt Bess.

Annie cut her curls off to her ears and put on Pap's woolen trousers and shirt. She buttoned the shirt all the way to the collar to hide that she had no Adam's apple. She'd convince the widow that she was the right man for the job, all right. Then she took James's Whitworth from the mantel, and the box of cartridges. She also took William's favorite book, the one he'd been reading to her when he left.

Stealing away with the late moon, she walked on through swamp and field. She passed gangs of Yanks, swarming like locusts across

Virginia, taking everything not tied down and burning the rest so no one else could have it. She hid at night, sleeping in the tops of trees. During the day, when she heard them coming she disappeared into a log, or a ravine, and once a tobacco field.

And when she finally reached Portsmouth, looking as ragged as any war-weary boy, she marched right up to the red brick home of Mrs. Margaret Trudeau. A large, bespectacled man opened the double doors. He wore a black suit, a white shirt with a black bow tie, and a clean mustache twisted neatly at the tips; even his fingernails were clean. He was a surefire dandy, never worked a hard day's work in his life.

"My name is James Anachie Gordon." Annie lifted her chin, looking him square in the eye, using her brother's name. "I'm healthy enough to fight, and I'll take your grandson's place."

Mrs. Trudeau was so relieved to see a body take the place of her grandson that she couldn't—or wouldn't—see the truth of Annie. She saw only a boy willing to fight. And the dandified lawyer—Mr. Wentworth—was too relieved that the deed was done. If either had seen through her disguise, she'd surely have been arrested.

But people see what they want to see.

There was no need to stay longer, no need to meet the grandson she had replaced, no need for any hospitality. The dandy offered the army contract to her, and Annie signed: *James Anachie Gordon.*

With a nod good-bye, Mrs. Trudeau promised to put the money into an account available to her after the war—as protection against Annie deserting her post, which would have the military come looking for her grandson.

The lawyer then grabbed a top hat and a frock coat, and led Annie to the back of the house, where a horse and carriage waited. Servants scurried out the back door with baskets of foodstuffs, packing the carriage.

And off they went.

She didn't look back. Her future was ahead of her, not behind.

The carriage eased around a bend in the road, passing a clump of trees.

"Hold up there!" boomed a bull-necked man, stepping from the shadows. "You're mightily brave coming to these parts, with blue-bellied Yanks crawling like snakes all about." The man was dressed in fading blue flannel with ragged green trim. Behind him stood two younger soldiers, dressed in similar uniforms, rifle-muskets aimed low at Annie and the lawyer. One tall and lanky fellow wore his cap cocked at an angle, red hair spilling from beneath its rim. His black pants seemed too short for his long legs, and his grin was as crooked as his cap. The other soldier was shorter, with broader shoulders, making him look more like a potato. This one had no shoes; his feet were wrapped in cloth.

"Hello, sergeant." Mr. Wentworth smiled. The smile startled Annie, for it seemed out of place on such a sullen face. "This here is James Anachie Gordon. We're here to see Major Owens, if you please. He's expecting us."

"So you finally reeled in a ripe one, did you?" The sergeant lifted his rifle. He looked at Annie, his brows knitted together as he took his full measure of James Gordon.

She held his stare, just as steady as his.

"And that"—Mr. Wentworth raised his voice, pointing to the baskets in the back of the carriage—"is for Company G, compliments of Mrs. Trudeau."

The burly sergeant scratched his chin, a smile spreading across his face. And the two younger soldiers suddenly came to life. If men could fly, they surely did at that moment. In two bounds and a whoop, they were on the back of the carriage. It lurched under their weight, and the horse neighed in protest.

"Good great glory, Pop!" the tall one hooted. "There's cake and apples! Figs and berry jam! And, Pop, there's coffee! *Real* coffee! I shall name my rifle after the fine Mrs. Trudeau, such a proper Southern lady as ever there was, Pop!"

The sergeant had to see for himself. Coffee was rare as gold these days. The carriage bounced as the sergeant jumped onto the back of it. Annie grinned. Mrs. Trudeau was leaving nothing to chance.

The three soldiers sniffed the coffee in long, lingering whiffs.

"Mr. Wentworth," said the sergeant, his smile now wide as the sky, "only an angel could find real coffee in these desperate times. You must send our greatest compliments to that wonderful and lovely Mrs. Trudeau."

"That I will, sergeant." Mr. Wentworth giddyupped the horse.

"Jiggers! They got shoes!" hooted the potato boy as he unbound his feet. His soles were callussed and bloodied, his nails black with rot. How the potato boy walked at all was an amazement.

"You know, son"—the sergeant eased behind Annie on the carriage. His breath smelled heavy with rotting onions—"you don't look old enough to leave your mama."

"No son is old enough to leave his mama," Annie said, keeping her eyes straight ahead, tightening her grip on her rifle.

"True enough," the sergeant replied. The old bear whistled then. "Why, is that a Whitworth? Mighty rarified and fine rifle, son. Can you shoot that thing?"

"Better than most," she said.

The three soldiers hooted, but the loudest was the sergeant's son. Even the lawyer had to smile. Annie looked at him. He seemed a different man.

"You ask me," the sergeant's son said, his mouth stuffed brimful with cake, "substitutes are shameful specimens of humanity, lower than a snake's belly. Not motivated by patriotism, their nature is to desert. Heard tell some regiments put them up front when marching into battle."

The potato boy chuckled, his mouth so stuffed it overflowed, dripping onto his new shoes.

"You don't look to be the deserting sort, James Anachie Gordon," the sergeant said.

"No, sir, " Annie said. "I am not. You can ask my mama."

The sergeant chuckled.

"Well, we'll have time aplenty to find the truth of that matter!" He slapped her shoulder none too gently. "My name is Gideon, and that scrawny stick is my son, Dylan. He's too young to leave his mama, too. The last one, with the big feet there, is Jasper. His mama is with the angels now. And this be the Ninth Virginia, Company G! Better known as the Portsmouth Rifles. We have a proud and mighty heritage, son. You have a lot to live up to."

CHAPTER FIVE

Finally, near day's end, the carriage crested a hill and rolled into the valley below. Stretching to the horizon stood row after row of white tents, all sparkling in the waning sun. Cavalry units still trotted around the tents. Everywhere columns of men marched and drilled, thousands of men. There were flags waving, drums beating, flutes playing, men shouting, guns firing, wagons rolling, horses neighing, mules braying, dogs barking.

Dylan and Jasper were catcalling to others, hootin' and hollerin' and showing off their new wares courtesy of Mrs. Trudeau. Some whooped and others waved as a flood of men walked, then ran, to greet them.

At first Annie flinched, thinking they were too close and might see her disguise. But no one paid her any heed as all eyes were on the barrels and baskets provided by Mrs. Trudeau. Most of the men were a sorry sight, as ragged, lean, and hungry as the potato boy. Good enough, Annie thought. With them being so concerned about their feet and stomachs, who's going to pay attention to her?

A tall, gaunt man with more hair on his chin than on his head stepped toward the carriage. His officer's uniform, no longer shiny, showed the tears and grime of too many battles.

"*Major* Owens!" Mr. Wentworth's smile was now full-faced as he jumped from the carriage to greet the man with a hearty shake. "John! You are looking as dapper as ever. Seems like the army life suits you!"

"Civilian life seems to go well for you. Have you finally comes to your senses about joining our cause?"

"We both know I can do more for our boys staying right where I am. As you can see. . . ." Mr. Wentworth pointed to the supplies.

Major Owens turned toward Annie. "This is the substitute for Margaret's grandson, I gather. That's one fancy rifle. A Whitworth, is it? How did you come by such a rifle, son?"

"My father bargained for it. It belonged to a captain in the Georgia cavalry. He liked my father's colt."

"That must have been some colt." Major Owens sucked in a whistle. "I suppose you can use that thing?"

"I've heard tell he's better than most, sir!" Gideon snapped to with a salute and a wily grin.

Mr. Wentworth pulled out Annie's papers from his inner coat pocket. "Here's his paperwork, John. I'm sure you'll find everything in order."

Major Owens took the papers. Without reading them, he signed, his pen sweeping in big, scrolling letters. He then boomed to Gideon, "Sergeant, see this recruit to his new home! Jarrod and I have some old times to catch up on!"

"Sir, if you don't mind." The sergeant's son, Dylan, stepped up with his own salute. "The Portsmouth Rifles have a fine and honorable reputation to uphold. Some of us have been here from the beginning, fighting proud in the Battle of Seven Pines, Second Manassas, Sharpsburg. Not too many flags fly as high as ours, sir, and well, we can't let just any strawfoot join us."

"What are you suggesting, private?"

Something's afoot. Annie tensed.

"Well, sir, a boast's been made," said Dylan. "Seems to me, it's our duty to see if'n this boy and his fancy rifle can live up to it."

"Jiggers," Jasper, the potato boy, snorted, and not too quietly.

Major Owens brushed his beard in thought. For a long while he looked at Annie, and not once did he blink. Annie looked to Dylan, then to Gideon. Each wore the same crooked grin. She looked to the lawyer, who rocked on his heels in amusement, then she looked back to the major, who smiled, equally amused. Then the major said, "You may have a point, private. Well, sergeant, see to it that Private Gordon lives up to that boast."

"Yes, sir!" Gideon slapped Annie's shoulder. "Follow me, son."

Gideon led her through the camp. As they passed a row of tents, more men began to fall into place behind them, hooting and hollering.

"Dylan's got himself another pigeon," someone shouted. There followed more hollers as others fell into line.

"Everyone knows Dylan's the best. Two bits say the strawfoot misses on the first shot!"

"That fancy rifle can tickle a bear's tail at fifteen hundred yards. He wouldn't be having the gun if'n he didn't know how to shoot it. My money's on the strawfoot!"

"Ah, that's a lot of rifle for a squirt. My money's on Dylan."

"You're on!" another shouted.

Finally the procession stopped in a pasture. Much of the grass had been trampled and small trees broken in half from the footfalls of the thousands of men and horses. But an old oak stood defiant, a target attached to its trunk. Behind it, at regular intervals, were posted other targets.

"That"—Gideon pointed to the oak—"is one hundred yards if it's an inch."

"It ain't the gun that matters, strawfoot. It's the one who's holding it." Dylan loaded his rifle-musket, and swung it up with a movement smooth as a hawk's glide. Planting his rear foot firmly, he closed an eye, inhaled with a sharp whistle, and fired. A moment later the target bounced as the bullet found its mark, sending a cloud of birds cackling in fright and rage.

Soldiers behind him yodeled, Jasper the loudest. Gideon scratched his chin, trying not too hard to hide his prideful smile.

Now Annie swung her Whitworth off her shoulder.

She reached for a cartridge from her belt, then poured powder down the barrel and, with the ramrod, drove the bullet home, every move deliberate and determined.

"Slow as molasses, you ask me. I'll double that wager the strawfoot misses!"

"Thank god it ain't a Yank comin', or we'd be dead for sure!" someone clucked.

Behind her, soldiers exchanged more coins, upping the ante. And the higher the ante, the louder the shouts. And the louder the shouts, the more men gathered to see what the ruckus was all about.

Annie cocked the hammer, breathing slow and even, dug in her foot.

"Target, sir?" Annie asked.

Gideon gave a nod. "Same tree, son. Sometime today, if you have a mind to. My bones are—"

Annie fired, a puff of white smoke circling her head.

Not a breath later, a branch exploded free from the trunk.

And the crowd exploded in whoops and hollers and more turkey dancing. The lawyer and the major were shaking hands in congratulations for a fair trade.

Dylan was already reloading his rifle-musket, his crooked grin suddenly straight.

"Target, Pop?" he swung his rifle up.

Gideon pointed to the next target. "See that tree with the two rags tied around the trunk? Two hundred yards!"

Dylan fired. Two breaths later, a branch above the rags shook with the impact.

Annie reloaded her Whitworth. She inhaled to steady herself, planted her foot again, stiffened her shoulder, then aimed and fired.

This time, the branch exploded.

And the crowd cheered. Even Mr. Wentworth whooped. Major Owens looked as pleased as if he had just eaten a slice of Mama's peach pie.

Dylan's scowl deepened as he reloaded.

"Target, Pop?" he spat, his voice close to cracking. Jasper snorted nervously. The crowd quieted, the silence thick as cold molasses.

Gideon pointed to the next target farther down the line, and boomed like artillery: "That tree with the red flags. That's five hundred yards!"

"Impossible shot," someone said.

Breathing slow and steady, Dylan eased down onto his knees and aimed. Slow and steady, steady . . .

He fired. And then a branch burst into pieces as the bullet hit its mark.

The crowd inhaled, but did not yet cheer. Instead, their heads snapped about as one, turning to Annie.

Annie reloaded her Whitworth. She looked to the target, taking into account how the bullet might arc through the sky. There was no breeze. If she aimed too high, the bullet would just fly overhead. If she aimed too low, it would bury itself in the dirt long before reaching the target.

Now she, too, eased to the ground, using her elbows to brace herself.

Dylan chuckled. "Mighty odd time to take a nap, stawfoot."

She flipped the sight up, closing one eye and focusing on another branch. She knew what she did next would set her place here in camp. If she missed the shot, Dylan would strut around like a cock rooster, crowing how great he was and slapping her shoulder. And then he'd forget her as just another pigeon in camp. Everyone else would forget her, as well. She would disappear into the crowd and become like everyone else.

She would know her place. *Know her place.* The words boiled inside her.

She moved the sight, focusing on a tree *behind* the five hundred mark, the one flagged at seven hundred yards.

"Seven hundred yards," she announced.

And then she fired, a puff of smoke curling from the barrel. Her shoulder rocked with the recoil, but a branch toppled with the impact.

And the crowd erupted like a summer cloudburst.

"Glad you're on our side!" Major Owens slapped Annie's back. Others, too, greeted her with yodels and handshakes. "Not sure how that rifle will work at close range, son. But by thunder, we'll find a way."

Dylan smiled, too, offering his hand. But Annie recognized that smile. She had seen it often enough on James to know that behind that honey sweetness stirred a bear, spoilin' for a fight.

"It's a different story when the target's coming at you," Dylan said.

Annie gripped his hand, and squeezed. That bear was a-growling fierce, and she meant to meet him head-on.

"True enough," she said, returning the smile.

CHAPTER SIX

Dylan sauntered like a young buck dancing proud in the springtime as he led her back to their tents. A few soldiers, those who took a chance and bet on the recruit, patted Annie's back in congratulations. Their day done, most of the soldiers meandered back to their tents, their cheers melting away. The spectacle was over for everyone but the strutting cock rooster.

"Seems like we're messmates, strawfoot." Dylan eased next to her. "Just so you know, nothing's settled, despite your mighty fine rifle there."

"Jiggers!" Jasper chuckled, his feet flopping hard on the ground, his new boots undone. "Haven't had that much fun in days."

Dylan shot him a glance, and the potato boy bit his lip in silence.

The pup tent was small. Just those two stretched out would fill it up. Any more than that, and they'd fit together like spoons in a drawer. Even when everyone slept with their clothes on, this was still too close for comfort for Annie.

"I'll stay outside," she said.

Dylan stretched out inside the tent like a yawning cat. "Suit yourself. Don't let the bedbugs bite. They're worse than the bears in these parts."

Annie didn't mind sleeping outside. Chewing on bread and apples, she leaned against a tree. Not everyone slept. Campfires sparkled like stars above the Blue Ridge. Somewhere a harmonica played "Home, Sweet Home."

Home, and Annie thought of Mama. She felt guilty for sneaking away like a common thief. Maybe she should've at least left a note. Maybe . . .

But then the old anger rose up like swampy bile. No. She did what she had to do. Even her brother William would have given his nod.

Somewhere a fiddle cooed like a mourning dove. Using her haversack as a pillow, she scratched her head, stretched out, and looked up at the sea of stars. There was comfort in those stars, William always said. They had camped out the night before he left, in their favorite place across the far pasture, a clearing tucked in a grove of elm. The earth rose in the center and was crowned with a giant live oak. They climbed to the top to touch the stars. From atop that oak, William told her of the North Star that sailors used to find their way home. "No matter where we go from here, no matter what happens, when you think of me, find the North Star, there! And I'll look up; we'll see it at the same time, and it'll be like we're side by side, just like right now." The next morning he waved good-bye as he disappeared into Pap's cornfield. She didn't know it would be his last good-bye, or she would have told him that he was her hero.

But she didn't tell him anything. She was too angry that he was leaving her behind. And she thought there was time enough to set things right.

The fiddle stopped playing, and the only sounds—besides Dylan's snoring—were the chirrups of crickets and the peepings of tree frogs. Annie took a long breath, and let it out slow.

Regret was a big apple to swallow.

Reveille sounded long before sunrise, but Annie was already up and about. She sought out the woods to do her business in private. By the time she returned to the campsite, Dylan was astir.

"A new day, strawfoot!" He slapped Annie on the shoulder. It seemed a little harder this time, and his grin a little sharper.

Jasper hacked deeply as he crawled out of the tent, and spat.

"Roll call!" Gideon boomed. He was stomping his way along the row of tents, rousing the men as he went along.

Annie stopped next to her haversack, and then she noticed her rifle was gone. Behind her, Dylan chuckled. She swung hard about to see him standing there, her Whitworth in hand. Behind him stood Jasper, holding his smile.

"Ain't no one tell you, strawfoot?" he asked. "This here rifle has been *conscripted* by the company's best, in service to Virginia."

For a moment she stood stone still, so angry it was hard to breathe. She thought to fight him but knew she couldn't, not like this, not with any hope of keeping her disguise. Instead she spat, a solid good spit, and aimed for Dylan's boots.

And she always hit her mark.

She wasn't one for tears; she'd give no one that satisfaction. Instead she aimed all her anger at him, just like she was aiming her rifle, making the shot deliberate and precise.

"This ain't over," she whispered.

"Course not, strawfoot. I'm a-counting on that," Dylan whispered back, and winked.

The men fell into formation, some without pants, some without shirts, all in disarray of some kind, spitting, grumbling, but each snapping to when his name was called.

"James Anachie Gordon." Annie snapped to attention when *his* name was called.

When roll call was finished, the men dispersed, and Annie turned on her heel. There again stood Dylan. He squared his shoulders and took a step forward.

But Annie wasn't moving, not this time.

"Boys." Gideon stepped up from behind and slapped his son. Seeing the Whitworth in Dylan's hands, he glanced at Annie. "Do we have a problem here?"

Gideon was watching her. Annie knew that complaining about the Whitworth would make her look like a tattletale, a weakling. And then they'd tease her, just like William and James had whenever she complained to Pap or Mama. Besides, living with James had given her plenty of practice on how to get even.

"No, *sir!*" she shouted.

"Don't call me sir." Gideon smiled in approval. "I work for a living. Glad to see you two getting along this fine morning!" The younger soldier gave his pap a smile. He smoothed back his bright red hair. Annie relaxed her shoulder and stepped aside. But all the while, she kept her eye fixed on Dylan. With a grunt, Gideon continued, "We'll be heading north in a short time, mark my word. Until then, we best be getting to the business of soldiering. Drill time, boys."

Tramp, tramp, tramp. Drilling seemed an easy thing to do, putting one foot in front of the other. But more than once Annie tripped, turned left instead of right, turned right instead of left. And with each misstep she took, Dylan howled. She squared her shoulders, and she took to more drilling. The quartermaster had issued her an Enfield to replace her musket. "Try not to lose this one," he chuckled. The Enfield was a mere spit of a gun compared to her Whitworth. And with every step, she wanted to spit all the more.

Jasper with his big potato feet walked as if his boots had shrunk.

"Better to have no shoes," Dylan chuckled.

"They're drilling us hard," Jasper whispered. "Your pop must be right. They'll be moving us soon."

Tramp, tramp, tramp.

As the sun rose higher, so did the heat. The Enfield grew heavier with every step, and her knapsack dragged her shoulders like dead weight, pinching her neck. Ahead, somewhere in the dust, the captain barked orders, echoed by Gideon's boom, and the column turned to the right, to the left, to the center. March! The hours—and the heat—rolled on.

Tramp, tramp, tramp!

When the bugle sounded the end of drill, Annie was bone weary, making a slow way back to her fire. There she found Gideon frying up vittles. From the smells of it, he'd put in a little bit of everything. Stronger still was the smell of coffee, strong enough to draw others of the Portsmouth Rifles about. There must have been a dozen chewing the fat about the fire.

"Potaters and corn pone, can't do better than that!" Gideon yodeled. Spying Annie, he raised a spoon in her direction. "You are a peculiar feller, James Anachie Gordon. Don't seem to smile much. But you held your own today, and that deserves a hearty meal!"

"Hear! Hear!" others raised their tin cups in salute.

Dylan and Jasper had spread a blanket out, each enjoying cake and jam, a tin of coffee, and a cigar. Dylan was busy cutting and shuffling cards with one hand. His eye kept sliding to the Whitworth, a mere touch away.

Dylan puffed a circle of smoke, which waddled like a duck before drifting into nothingness. Jasper squealed, like a pig's chuckle, even as he wheezed from the smoke.

Annie coughed.

Dylan offered a cigar to her.

"That's a homemade smoke, son." Gideon grinned and scratched his chin. "Don't rightly know what we put into it. But it'll put hair on your chest, by thunder."

Annie took the cigar, rolling it between her fingers. Her eye on Dylan, she raised the cigar to her pursed lips. She didn't like the taste of it, but she liked the freedom of it. Aunt Bess would be downright fitified to see her smoke. Mama would turn away in shame. William, on the other hand, would slap his knees in appreciation.

Then she inhaled. She meant to puff a circle, do one better than Dylan, and bigger. But the cigar tasted rancid like swamp water, burning her throat.

"Jiggers," Jasper breathed.

Suddenly her lungs squeezed as she wheezed for breath.

Dylan hooted, taking back the cigar before she dropped it.

"It's an acquired taste." He leaned back, puffing another circle. "For the refined palate."

Annie wheezed, her stomach threatening to squeeze out its meal and then some. Gideon offered her a tin of water. Her eyes burning, her nose watering, she gulped the water in hopes of putting out the fire. Gideon turned back to his cooking, his body shaking with laughter.

Dylan smacked his lips. "Have to admit, Pop, it is curious that Mrs. Trudeau has managed to gather such fineries in the midst of so much lacking."

"Son, let it be said that there is nothing gentle about the gentler sex. It is prolly best for us to never know how it was done, but be grateful that it was."

"Hear! Hear!" Jasper raised his tin cup.

Annie drank more water, and the burn finally eased. Then she reached inside her haversack to pull out William's book.

Yep, William would still be hooting.

"You read, son?" Gideon asked.

"It's my brother's favorite book, sir. About a man called the Deerslayer, who believed that every living thing should follow the gifts of its nature."

Gideon puffed and gave a nod. "Sounds like a good book, son."

"Yeah, William taught me to read. I taught him to shoot."

"Well, that sounds promising, if'n he shoots anything like you."

"Not too promising." She coughed. "He was killed at Manassas. And I don't read all that well. Always had better things to do, I guess."

Gideon removed his cap and crossed himself in quick prayer.

"Read to us from your brother's book, son." Gideon eased to the ground. He relit his pipe, and puffed smoke rings.

The others quieted, too, cocking one ear in her direction. Even Dylan and Jasper listened. Annie read, and in the words she saw William. Annie chanced a glance skyward to find the North Star, and found a bit of comfort there.

PART THREE

GRACE

CHAPTER SEVEN

June 1863

All of Gettysburg was in a perfect uproar. Townsfolk were rushing up and down the road, their shouts lost in the clamor of wheels, horses, and even occasional gunfire.

Pappa had been gone since early morning, and hadn't told anyone where he was going. Mamma was fit to be tied. It was all Grace could do to stay out of her way. So when Mamma needed peaches delivered to Miss Mary, Grace was jumping happy to oblige.

Grace knew every road, every trail, every alley into town, and knew how to slip through them all without being seen. After all, she and Millie had done it plenty of times.

Grace walked fast along the road.

"You, child!" someone hailed her as a wagon pulled up behind her. She swerved and looked up to see Mrs. Butler smiling down at her. The wind played with the feathers dangling from Mrs. Butler's large round hat, tickling the woman's nose and chin. She pushed the feathers aside with an angry flip of her hand. "Where you heading, child?"

"I'm delivering some peaches to Miss Mary," Grace said.

Mr. Butler fiddled with the reins, keeping the horses in check, looking as uncomfortable as a boy whose shoes fit too tight. Mr. Butler was not so tall as Pappa, but big as a bear all the same.

"Hey, Mr. Butler," smiled Grace.

"Hey, Gracie." Mr. Butler returned the smile. He and Pappa often swapped stories.

Pappa liked Mr. Butler. It didn't matter to Pappa that Mr. Butler was white. And it didn't matter to Mr. Butler that Pappa was black. But Grace suspected it mattered to Mrs. Butler, just like it mattered to Mamma.

"How's your pap?" Mrs. Butler shrilled. Mrs. Butler took pride in knowing everyone's business, Mamma always said. Mrs. Butler might not think much of Pappa, but it was no secret she thought a lot of his land, and his orchard, and his barns. "You ask me, there isn't going to be one Negro left in town by the end of the month—except perhaps your pap."

"Pappa isn't going anywhere," Grace said. "This is our home. Just like it's your home, Mrs. Butler. You going to have some cowardly rebel chase you off? Well, no one is chasing us off our land."

"I commend your courage." Mr. Butler smiled, clicking his tongue. "You tell your pap I said hey, and I'll be by soon enough!"

Mrs. Butler coughed in a fluster as Mr. Butler giddyupped the horses.

And Grace, too, dashed off, careful not to spill her basket.

Grace found Miss Mary standing on her stoop, watching the crowd on the streets. It seemed the whole town, what was left of it, had gathered here. Miss Mary offered a worried smile as she took the basket from Grace.

"What's happening, Miss Mary?" asked Grace. "Why is everyone so up in craziness?"

"Good great glory, Grace, there!" Miss Mary pointed southward.

Grace gasped. The southern sky was all aglow.

Miss Mary wailed, "It's true, the rebs are coming! And they're burning everything in their way!"

"I have to go home straightaway! I have to get back to Mamma." Grace began to dash off, but Miss Mary caught her.

"It's too late now, Gracie. You're not going anywhere this night." Miss Mary shook her head. "You'll stay with me until we know what's going on out there. Then tomorrow I'll send word to your Pappa."

Grace looked to the glowing southern sky. *The rebs are coming.* The words rattled like a crow's caw. *And they're burning everything in their path!*

CHAPTER EIGHT

Her worry ate her from the inside out. For the longest while, Grace tried to be still, thinking she could trick sleep into coming. But all night her foot tap-tap-tapped the air.

Tap, tap, tap. Millie didn't say goodbye.

Tap, tap, tap. The rebs were coming.

Tap, tap, tap. Mamma must have fretted all night when Grace didn't get home. And Pappa must not have come home, because if he had, he would have come into town to look for her, and the first place he would've looked would be here.

Grace curled in the heavy upholstered chair nearest the front window, breathing in the breeze and the night-blooming jasmine. Grace liked this window. She could see who was coming into town from here.

All night wagons were rolling and horses neighing, dogs barking and neighbors shouting. The southern sky burned brighter than the moon.

The embers glowed in the fireplace, throwing a dull red glow about the room. Crawling off the chair, Grace threw a log on the fire and watched the embers spit themselves awake.

Just then, noises came from the kitchen.

"I know you are awake, child," Miss Mary called. "Come help me with the baking. Busy hands are the best way to stay any worry."

"I'm worried for Mamma." Grace walked into the kitchen, the floor cold on her bare feet.

"Of course you are, child. But no need for us to worry just this moment. It was Emmitsburg that burned last night, and not because of any Confederate invasion. Some old fool got carried away in panic and burned down twenty-seven houses. Families lost everything they had on this earth because an old fool jumped at his own shadow. Foolishness, that's all it was."

"Everyone is in such a panic." Mary's sister, Martha Scott, emerged from the back stairs into the kitchen. She was tall and stoop-shouldered, rail thin like a cornstalk, with her brown hair pulled tightly back on her head. No two sisters were more different than Miss Mary and Mrs. Scott.

"Good morning, Mrs. Scott," Grace offered.

"It's not morning yet. I haven't gotten a good night's sleep in days, Mary." Mrs. Scott tied on her apron. She moved past Grace as she went for the large pot simmering on the back of the cast-iron stove. "You see that rabble out there? Most of those Negroes are leaving, but they're not alone. Our own men are skedaddling. I heard the postmaster is hiding in the woods. Being a Republican, he fears capture as much as those Negroes. Something's coming for sure, Mary."

"But not today, Martha." Miss Mary raised her voice, glancing at Grace. Miss Mary cleared her throat, then said, "The major is calling for a town meeting at the diamond this morning. And Governor Curtis sent another telegram, calling for fifty thousand volunteers."

"Well, that explains why so many of the young men are leaving. I tell you, the world is about to explode something terrible." Mrs. Scott checked the griddle cakes in the warmer.

Someone rapped on the back door of the kitchen.

"Who on earth would come this early? Mary, be careful."

Miss Mary nodded at her sister, drying her hands on her apron as she eased Grace out of sight. She stood still for a moment, and then asked, "Who's there?"

"A Friend, with a friend."

"Friend Alice?" Miss Mary heaved a sigh, opening the door just far enough to let three shadows—a woman and two girls—slip into the kitchen. "God keep you! I can't believe you made it this far! People in these parts don't like Quakers, especially now!"

Grace had heard stories about the Quakers, how they helped slaves run away to freedom up north. Southerners hanged them as thieves. Northerners called them trouble-makers.

Grace fixed her eyes on the smallest shadow. As the shawl fell from her head, Grace could see a girl not much older than herself. She had deep ebony skin and eyes as brown and round as a doe's, a scar cutting across one cheek and another across her neck. Her hands looked like Pappa's hands, hard and gnarled, as she clutched the shawl tight about her shoulders.

"My apologies for surprising you like this, Mary." Friend Alice removed her straw hat. Her eyes, blue as a summer sky and round as the moon, fell on Grace and smiled. Grace shivered under their sparkle. The woman turned back to Mary. "We were just arrived in Mercersburg when word came of the burning in Emmitsburg. All night we were in the woods. I'm sure no one saw us. I thought it safer to come here straightaway rather than to move on to the mill. Some rebels have destroyed the tracks and the dam at Rock Creek. Rebel parties are raiding all up and down the ridges. It's truly frightful out there."

"There's so much commotion everywhere." Miss Mary looked quickly up and down the road before shutting the door. "Come, come. I'll take you downstairs. There's no telling who is watching now."

Miss Mary led them to the kitchen cupboard and removed a plank, revealing a door. The door creaked as it opened. Grace exhaled: *a secret stairwell!*

"Grace, bring some food and some blankets. Mrs. Scott, make some hot tea for our guests." Miss Mary ushered them down the dark stairs.

Her sister watched the procession, looking none too happy. And when Miss Mary disappeared into the secret cellar, she hissed, "I do declare, Mary doesn't think about us, not at all. The rebels are coming and look what she brings into the house." Mrs. Scott scowled. Grace smiled one of Pappa's smiles, the crooked one he'd give to Mamma when her words spewed like steam from a tea kettle. He'd stand there, knowing that anything he said wouldn't be right enough. With another hiss, Mrs. Scott shoved a bowl of peaches and biscuits toward Grace.

"This war," Mrs. Scott went on, turning back to the oven. "Everything is *their* fault."

"Pappa always said," Grace said, steadying the peaches, "there are possibilities, here in Gettysburg. It's what makes Gettysburg home."

"There won't be a town left after all this," Mrs. Scott harrumphed.

Grace slipped into the secret stairwell, the stairs creaking with her footfalls. Reaching the dirt floor, she held her breath. The thick rock walls smelled musky like mushrooms. The cellar was dark as a cave, except for a lantern glow at the back of the room. She walked through a maze of empty barrels and crates, moving toward that glow. As she came closer to the wall, she noticed that some of the stones had been removed to reveal a hidden room. And in that secret room sat the two girls. Friend Alice stood next to Miss Mary.

Miss Mary took the bowl from Grace, and offered it to the older girl.

"Grace!" That very moment, a familiar voice boomed above in the kitchen. The boards above their heads trembled with every stomping heavy footfall, dirt raining down on their heads.

"Pappa!" Grace shouted. Pappa was already bounding down the stairs and racing across the floor. Without missing a step, he scooped Grace into his arms.

"We was worried, baby girl, but I told Mamma, Miss Mary will take you in. Miss Mary—" He stood to face Miss Mary and extended his hand to offer a firm shake. "The rebels have been sighted on the mountain."

"They're coming, Mr. Bryan, to be sure," Friend Alice said.

"Friend Alice?"

Grace stared at Pappa. Pappa knew where the hidden stairs were! He knew where the cellar was! *Pappa knew Friend Alice?*

Then Pappa turned, stooping low to see inside the secret room, taking notice of the two figures huddled there. He took his hat off and offered an easy smile in greeting.

He knew because he helped runaways, too.

Did Mamma know? Was that why she seemed angry all the time? And so afraid?

Grace smiled, big and bold and stubborn. Just like Pappa.

PART FOUR

TILLIE

CHAPTER NINE

Saturday, June 20

Tillie looked up, her heart full to bursting to hear the church bells ringing in the distance. She meant to take full advantage of her freedom. No studying, no baking bread for the church, no washing clothes or tearing rags, and certainly no sewing!

She ran straightaway to the diamond, where what was left of the town had already gathered to watch the volunteers. Just then, shouting arose. Men too old to volunteer had assembled on the diamond in the center of town. Some men were dressed in ancient uniforms. Some wore farmer overalls, others their Sunday best. But all the men were armed with something: a rusted musket, an old sword, shovels, pitchforks, pickaxes.

Before the assembly stood a portly man, his jacket buttoned tight about his middle. He shouted orders, and everyone marched—each in his own direction. This way and that, they stumbled through the maneuvers.

Tillie chuckled.

Tillie stayed for a while longer, reluctant to go home.

"Tillie!" Mother's sharp voice greeted her. "Help me with these loaves, child. Watch that you don't knead the bread too much."

Father straightened in his chair. He set the newspaper down, looking to Mother. "The governor is calling for more volunteers."

"I'm so tired of this." Mother punched her dough so hard, the table trembled. "Everyone is at their wits' end. I can almost understand how that poor old man in Emmittsburg lost his sensibility. First the rebels are coming. Then the rebels are not coming. Raiding parties scourge the countryside—some were in Waynesboro, twenty miles down the road. It's all so bedeviling, everyone has lost their sense. And where's our troops? Our most able men from the college and seminary are gone to Harrisburg to volunteer. Who's left to protect us? It's too much, I tell you, too much."

"Calm yourself, Mother," Father said. "The volunteers from the local mounted defense are patrolling the Pike. They're keeping an eye on things."

"Besides, the rebels won't come here, Mother," Tillie said, sliding another loaf from the oven. "Don't you doubt that at all; our boys won't let them."

"Your head is in the clouds, Tillie." Mother shook her head. "And one day you'll fall to earth, landing full on your backside."

Rebels wouldn't dare come to Gettysburg, Tillie thought, no matter what others said. *Our handsome and noble troops will push those traitorous scoundrels back where they belong!*

CHAPTER TEN

At morning light everyone gathered at the diamond again, including Mother and Father.

"A large rebel force has been seen in the mountains!" Burgess Robert Martin boomed, his voice carrying across the diamond.

Tillie inhaled sharply, looking to Father. He rocked on his heels as he stroked his beard. Father was too old to be accepted by the army, and he didn't like it that he was stuck here in Gettysburg while others went off to fight. He considered Jefferson Davis a traitor to the United States, and traitors should be hanged. That's what Father said.

Tillie saw Jennie across the way, standing with her mother. She saw her teacher, Mrs. Eyster, looking every bit as worried as her mother. She saw Miss Mary and Mrs. Scott. Even Mr. Scott was here.

And standing near Miss Mary was—who was that? Grace Bryan? Why, Grace Bryan looked positively fretful. Poor Grace. Tillie shook her head. Every night more and more of the town's Negroes left, taking with them only what they could carry on their backs, stumbling under the weight of their bundles. If they spilt their belongings in their stumbling, they left them where they fell, pressing on in panic. The streets were littered with abandoned goods, and the piles had been picked through by others.

Tillie looked about for Grace's father. There was no sign of Abraham Bryan.

Everyone was talking about him. It wasn't safe to be so uppity.

No matter how good a farmer he was, how much land he owned, how good his peaches were, there were still some things that just weren't proper.

"We need volunteers to ride to Cashtown Gap and cut some trees to block the rebels' way," the burgess declared.

Father was deep in thought. Suddenly he stepped forward.

"No!" Mother shook her head.

"Dearest." Father patted her shoulder. "All day you bake bread for the church, for the volunteers, and for the ladies' circle. You make linen bandages, and sew flags, and knit socks—you do something that matters! I do nothing but read the newspaper. This is my chance to help."

"Husband." Mother wept. "Your place is with us. You take care of us! Tillie, tell him!"

Father kissed Mother's cheek in good-bye. "I'll be back before you know it."

He patted Tillie's head, just as he had done when she was small. His smile was brighter and bigger than Tillie had seen it in a long while.

"Don't fret so, Mother," Tillie said. "Like Father said, they'll be back soon enough."

Tillie walked Mother home, their arms linked together. "Oh, child," Mother sighed. "To be your age and without a worry." Mother stared out across the town toward the mountains.

At home, Tillie helped Mother bake biscuits, sifting the flour, carefully adding salt and water. She sank her hand into the mix, just like Mother had shown her, and squeezed it through her fingers. The stuff was more like gruel than dough.

"Looks like too much water," her mother said. "You forgot the lard. And you need more flour."

It might have made for a long day, waiting for Father, but it was barely noon when she heard the sound of pounding hoofs. She followed Mother outside. The volunteers had returned! Father was with them!

"We were too late," Father wheezed as he dismounted. The horse was foaming from the hard gallop. "Lee's entire army has crossed the Potomac. The rebels had already crossed the pass. We didn't get half-way there when we saw them! We came so close, they fired at us. We need to think about leaving town, Mother. The rumors are true! *The rebels are on their way to Gettysburg!*"

PART FIVE

ANNIE

Wednesday, June 24

CHAPTER ELEVEN

It had been a long and wearisome march from Suffolk to the Potomac River. It was only two and a half feet deep, only 150 yards wide, but on the other side was a whole different world. Behind her, the earth had been scorched of life. But there, on the other side of the river, for as far as she could see, was green heaven. An orchard spread up rolling hills, surrounded by fields of corn and wheat.

"Jiggers," Jasper whispered in awe. "Ain't that some milk and honey paradise?"

"Plenty ripe for the taking!" Dylan spat.

"Don't seem right," Annie whispered. "They have all that, so why take everything we had?"

"Ain't nothing right about this war, strawfoot," Dylan chuckled. "Since when does that count for anything? Ain't right them blue-bellies burned down everything my pap had, everything you had. Ain't nothing right about what's going on, but here it is."

The orders came down, and Gideon trumpeted, "*Cross the river!*"

Annie began unlashing her boots.

"That don't seem wise," Jasper told her. "Water seems cold enough to freeze your toes."

"Maybe." Annie swung her boots over her shoulder. "But good boots are as rare as good coffee these days, and don't you know that? This water ain't near as cold as the creek back home, and I aim to keep my boots!"

But she was wrong about the water; its cold sent shivers right through her. The cold forced her to double-quick march across the river. And she wasn't alone, as everyone soon broke ranks, churning the water into mud as the soldiers crossed pell-mell.

Reaching the other side, they marched in columns along the narrow roadway, moving into the rolling hills, through the orchards, where she helped herself to cherries and peaches. She passed huge barns that made Pap's barn seem a toy.

Then the Portsmouth Rifles marched into Chambersburg. It was as fine a town as Annie had ever seen, with old, bent trees lining the roads and brick houses as large as the home of the widow Trudeau. Two grand hotels crowned the downtown road, and every balcony was crowded with people, watching them march into town.

People were everywhere, along the road, hanging out their windows, standing on their porches. The whole town had come out to see them. But the folks stood like scarecrows, their gazes sullen.

Bursting from the crowd, a trio of young boys hurled rotted peaches and cabbages at the soldiers. The soldiers broke their line to chase them down.

Annie marched past a little girl, hair like dirty sunshine, standing in the roadside mud clinging to a headless doll. She had moon-round eyes, and little ringlets about her face. She wore no shoes or stockings, the lace of her dress was ripped, and the dress hung loose. She reminded Annie of her little sister, and she almost smiled at the thought.

"Murderer!" A woman rushed up to the little girl, wrapping her arms about her. The woman looked as wretched and starved as the little girl.

Annie turned away.

Marching through the town, they bivouacked next to the railroad tracks.

"Sons of Virginia," Gideon called out, "we got chores to do!"

Dylan howled, leading a charge against the railroad ties, swinging a pickax high and wide. Others joined in, and the howling became a mighty roar that bounced off the clouds. The soldiers danced in a strange cotillion, hacking and tearing, burning what they couldn't hack and tear.

Annie was used to doing hard chores. But she wasn't used to doing such reckless, feckless destruction.

"Can't see much sense in this." Annie stood sentry, barely able to breathe with the smoke curling about their heads. "Not after what we seen back home."

"Can't understand why the Lord put curl in a pig's tail," Dylan hooted in reply. "We got our orders. I suppose there's reason enough."

Her stomach squeezed so hard, she heaved. And it all came up at once, her morning fixings and the cherries she had stolen. She heaved again, a rush of bile. And then she heaved again, falling to her knees, until it seemed not a speck of life was left in her.

CHAPTER TWELVE

"New orders, sons of Virginia!" Gideon hailed his troops. "Sweep the town and surrounding fields for supplies!"

"You're with me, strawfoot," Dylan chuckled, "if'n you can stand up straight now." He pointed down the road.

Annie knew that grin well enough by now: like some stubborn bear, he meant to continue his sparring. As swampy as she felt, Annie grinned back, holding her Enfield at the ready.

Working in groups of two and three, the Ninth Virginia joined the other regiments, sweeping down the street, through the gardens and kitchen houses and stables, gathering chickens and pigs and whatever food they could find.

The three of them—Dylan in the lead, with Jasper and Annie at his heels—came to a brown brick house. Surrounded by a wooden fence, its front yard was a once-tidy garden now overrun with weeds and chickens. Chickens!

Dylan hooted and gave chase. Jasper, too, and each soon caught a chicken.

"Don't need to take everything," Annie told them. "Leave something so they can eat, too."

Dylan and Jasper looked at her, then at each other, confused.

"Jiggers," Jasper snorted. "Ain't you hungry for some of the sergeant's special fried chicken?"

"Everyone's hungry," Annie insisted, remembering the little girl by the road.

"Strawfoot's right." Dylan let loose his chicken.

But no sooner did the chicken flit away than another soldier swooped in to catch it.

"Ain't that some pitiable sight," someone chuckled from the walkway. Two soldiers stood next to them. One, wearing a loose-fitting lieutenant's uniform, was a rakish sort, not much older than Dylan and not much taller, wearing a smile that was more sword-like than friendly. "The famous Dylan Good-Shot can't catch a stupid cluck?"

"Well, time's been good to you, Gabriel. Looks like your pap bought you a new uniform." Dylan returned the same sword-sharp smile. "Might need to have your mama sew it up proper to get a better fit."

"Watch your tongue." The soldier behind them shoved Annie aside as he returned to his comrades on the walkway, the chicken clucking and flapping frantically in his arms. "Show some respect, private, or we'll arrest your sorry face for insubordination."

"Jiggers," Jasper whispered. "This is gonna turn real bad real fast."

"Who are they?" Annie whispered back.

"They're part of the Fiftieth Georgia, from the southern part of the state. Been a long feud between the Fiftieth and the Ninth, about who's top dog and all."

"So?"

"Them's also Dylan's folk, from his mam's side. Real bad blood between the families."

Just then, from within the house, someone screamed. A bloodcurdling, end-of-life scream. Like the one her sister had screamed when some Yank stormed through their front door.

Annie should have thought about what she might do next. If she was arrested for insubordination or sedition, she'd be found out. But then the scream rent the air again, and she bolted toward the front door.

"James!" Dylan raced after her.

"Aw, jiggers!" Jasper ran after them.

"You there!" The lieutenant—Gabriel—called after them. "No one gave you leave. What goes on here is not your concern!"

"James!" Dylan shouted again, beating Annie to the door. "I thought we had this settled. You're with me, not the other way around."

Dylan in the lead, the three charged through the door. And just as quick, they rocked to a halt.

The room was a shambles. A large hutch had been tipped over, shattering its contents and spewing broken dishes and glassware across the floor. Its drawers had been pulled out and emptied. Annie suspected the soldiers had found what they were after: the family silver.

The soldiers had taken their sabers and shredded the high-backed chairs and the paintings on the wall. Vases, keepsakes, everything. Destroyed.

Standing the middle of the mayhem, a girl no taller than spring wheat whimpered as she clung to her mama's skirts. Her mama whimpered, too, her shoulders shaking in the effort to stay calm. The two watched Annie and Dylan.

"Please," the woman whispered, pointing. "My son . . ."

On the other side of the room, a soldier held a boy by the collar. The boy hung limp in the grasp, his face swollen from a beating.

"Didn't you hear me, *private*?" Gabriel stormed through the door, holding a pistol. "This is not your concern."

"I believe you started this conversation, *sir*." Dylan raised the Whitworth threateningly. "Looks like some things don't change, no matter what fancy duds you wear. You beating up women and children again, *sir*?"

"This here Northern whore is a criminal," Gabriel began. "She's guilty of hiding fugitives. . . ."

"You find any slaves hiding in those drawers, did you?" Annie hissed.

"You calling me a liar, *private*?" Gabriel stepped up so close to Annie, she could smell the onion he had for breakfast. Gabriel pointed to the woman. "She's a spy for the Federals."

Dylan exploded, pummeling the lieutenant's arm with the butt of the Whitworth. The pistol fired with the impact, and the woman and child screeched. The bullet struck the wall.

"Run!" Annie shouted to them. The woman gathered the limp body of her son and her daughter, and fled the house.

The second soldier—Drake, the one who'd caught the chicken—now pulled his pistol on Dylan. Annie rushed forward. At the same time,

Jasper yelled and balled his fists, and the two rammed into the man like riled-up bulls. All three exploded through the front door, rolling in a heap of howls.

Annie was used to hunting possum, and *this* chicken fighter was not near as bright as the possums she hunted that played dead for a living. As Drake struggled to his feet, Annie swung up, and with a wallop caught him under the chin, sending him sprawling backward. Jasper howled, jumping atop the man, pinning him down. Drake responded with a heave, losing his breakfast.

"Jiggers!" Jasper jumped. "Not on my new boots!"

The man struggled to get up, but Annie was faster.

"Just so you know, I don't ever miss my mark." She grabbed his pistol and aimed. "You hold still, or you'll see firsthand the truth of my boast."

Another shot rang out from inside. Annie and Jasper swerved as Dylan and the lieutenant tumbled through the front door.

"You always did hide behind your pap, you low-bred coward," Gabriel shouted as he swung his fist. Dylan caught it and returned the favor.

By now, others had heard the shots and the shouting, and raced toward the house to see what the ruckus was all about. They joined the fray, swinging fists and insults as fast as bullets. Soon the melee spread into the road.

Suddenly several shots rang out. Dylan and Gabriel stopped; Annie and Jasper ducked, covering their heads. Some fell to the ground in quick surrender, while others scattered like chickens on the run.

"Atten-SHUN!" It was Gideon and other sergeants who had fired their rifles. Next to them stood Major Owens and a captain from the Fiftieth Georgia.

The soldiers in the yard snapped to their feet and saluted.

"You men here"—Major Owens pointed to Dylan, Jasper, and Annie, and then Gabriel and Drake—"you stay put. The rest of you report back to wherever you came from." He turned to Dylan. "You think we have nothing better to do than fight among ourselves? Maybe we should confine you to solitary. What do you think, captain?"

The captain smiled in reply, but he flashed a pointed glance toward Gideon. Annie had to fight to hold down her grin.

"It would seem our boys are itching for a fight," Major Owens continued. "May I remind you, we are not ruffians. We do not beat up women and children. I'll leave your men in your expert hands, captain, to do with as you see fit. I'll tell the colonel when I see him."

The captain snapped a salute, calling out for Gabriel and Drake to fall in line. Gideon shot a pointed look at the captain, watching them quick-step back toward camp.

"Boyos, let's call it a day." Gideon turned back to Dylan.

"All this because of a chicken." Jasper scrubbed the scum from his boots. "Jiggers."

PART SIX

GRACE

CHAPTER THIRTEEN

Friday, June 26

Pappa was a mountain, but Mamma's worry had chipped away at the mountain with the steady force of wind and rain. Lee's army had crossed the Potomac, made its way through Chambersburg, and now moved across the pass. Raiders had been sighted as close as eight miles west of town.

Mamma's fears boiled over; Pappa *had* to do something. It was decided: he was putting Mamma and Grace on the train. But—and on this he stood solid as rock—he was not leaving. He had work to do. Grace wondered if Pappa's work had to do with Friend Alice and the two runaways.

Grace wanted to stay with Pappa. But both Mamma and Pappa would have none of it: she was leaving with Mamma.

The last of the town also meant to leave, everyone desperate to get away.

A woman pushed between them as she urged her children through the rail cars. "Be still! Be quiet!" And Mamma's hold on her slipped.

"I'm here, Mamma!" Grace shouted, but her shouts were lost as a boy dashed by her, followed quickly by three more in chase, spinning her around like a top. Another woman whirled hard about, holding tight to one child and balancing another on her hip. "Ruffians!" the woman shouted, pushing Grace back between two seats.

"Mamma!" Grace called. But Mamma was lost somewhere well

ahead of her in the crowd. She struggled to stand up, but a man bent with age shoved her against a seat. The train whistle blew, and Grace herself was ready to blow.

Pappa wouldn't be moved, and here she was being shoved about like a sack of apples. Well! Good glory almighty then, she wouldn't be moved either!

There was no second thought, no second-guessing, no confusion. Just that quick, Grace slipped through the door and jumped onto the platform. The whistle blew again, the stack huffing and puffing like some iron monster as the train moved away.

"Child!" a familiar voice shouted. Grace swallowed hard, steeling herself as she faced Miss Mary. Miss Mary, stubborn as Pappa and angry as Mamma, wasn't about to let her go. "Don't think you can get away, child."

"This is home." Grace tried to pull away. "Pappa won't be moved. You won't be moved. I won't be moved! I'm going home to help Pappa. He'll be mad," Grace said, "but not for long."

"I imagine he just might," Miss Mary said. "But he can only be upset with you if you're alive and well. I'll send word to him that you're staying with me tonight. Lordy, you are a handful."

Friend Alice had left the day before to scout for help, promising to return by nightfall. She still hadn't come back for the runaways. Everyone knew what that meant: she was trapped somewhere, a prisoner, or maybe killed.

"*They'll* be the death of us!" Mrs. Scott pointed to Grace as she stormed from the room. "You should get her and the other two out of here while you can, Mary. Think of us, for goodness' sake!"

Grace recognized that look Miss Mary gave to Mrs. Scott. Mamma gave that very same shame-on-you look to her all the time these days.

Miss Mary gave Grace a bowl filled with biscuits and peaches. "You can start earning your keep by taking these to our guests downstairs. The little one is Weezy. Her sister's name is Sorry."

"Those are funny names," Grace said. "Why would a mamma name her children so oddly?"

"Move along now, Grace," Miss Mary said.

Grace took the bowl and hurried down the secret stairs. "Hello," she said as she moved the plank shutter aside.

The smaller one, Weezy, smiled an easy, toothy smile as she took the bowl from Grace. Her sister, Sorry, didn't smile. Her face had not a whit of life, as if it had walked out one day and never returned. She just looked at everything, at everyone—and at no one. Not even as she took the bowl from Weezy.

Grace wondered where they'd been and what they'd seen. She imagined they'd come a long way, because they looked as ragged as the scarecrow on Pappa's field. But she said nothing and left them in the dark.

Miss Mary was waiting for her in the kitchen.

"I have to go home," Grace said.

"I sent the Jackson boy with word that you're here. I'm sure your pappa is on his way."

"He's going to be angry." Grace inhaled with a whistle.

"We all have consequences to bear for the choices we make," Miss Mary chuckled. "The question is, are the consequences worth the choice you made?"

Grace straightened her shoulders.

But the day ended soon enough, and Pappa still had not come for her.

The next morning, Miss Mary kept Grace busy with chores and away from the front window. Hour after hour, Pappa still didn't come for her. And Friend Alice didn't return for the runaways. Grace found a new worry, wondering if this was the same worry Mamma felt all the time: waiting for something to happen.

Now, preparing dinner for the runaways, she heard shouts outside. Grace raced to the front window.

"Maybe it's Pappa!" she shouted.

"Wait, child!" Miss Mary caught Grace's arm, and the two stood on the stoop.

"See, there they go again." Mrs. Scott flailed her arm. "No wonder the town is a basket of nerves. You almost want the rebels to get here, just to be done with it."

Watching the road, Grace shook her head. "Pappa . . ."

"All's well." Miss Mary forced a smile.

But it wasn't true.

"Miss Mary!" She pointed. Soldiers on horseback, in wagons, and on foot, in tight formation, were marching down Chambersburg Street. She couldn't tell from the ragged uniforms who they were, rebel or Union.

Neighbors, the few who'd stayed in town, poured into the streets to watch. Officers brandished their swords as the soldiers fired their guns into the air.

Miss Mary whirled on her heel as the Jackson boy ran past them.

"It's the rebs," he shouted. "General Early's taking over the town!"

CHAPTER FOURTEEN

The rebels were here!

And the moment was more terrible than anyone could have imagined.

"You can't be here, Grace." Miss Mary pushed Grace inside.

"Miss Mary"—Grace shook her head in disbelief—"*Pappa was wrong. The rebels are coming to take us away!*"

"Mary." Mrs. Scott herself could scarcely breathe. "They're just around the corner. If they find the runaways, they'll shoot us on the spot. I heard stories of neighbors burning neighbors out once they found out they were hiding them runaways."

"Then keep your mouth shut so no one will find out," Miss Mary hissed, bolting the front door. Mrs. Scott bit her lip. Miss Mary straightened her shoulders and said, "If they come in, we give them whatever they ask for. Foods, stores, blankets. We give them the family silver, Martha, do you hear? Seems to me, you be nice to a man with a gun, and he won't shoot. You give them what they ask for, and they have no reason to look for anything else. Meanwhile, Grace, we have to hide you."

Miss Mary took hold of Grace's arm and led her down the hidden stairs to the cellar. Frantic, she removed the stones and planks. "Grace, we need to keep you safe. This will be uncomfortable with the three of you packed in there like crackers. But it's only for a little while. And we can do anything for a little while, right?"

Grace gave a shallow nod as she squeezed her way into the room.

Sorry and Weezy looked frightened, holding each other. Grace felt the same fear growing in her own belly.

"Pappa?" Grace said before Miss Mary closed the door.

"He's fine," Miss Mary said, already covering the doorway. "We'll hold to that thought until we're told otherwise. No need bringing more trouble on our shoulders just yet. God keep you safe, all three of you."

Miss Mary replaced the wooden shutter and the daylight disappeared. Grace heard the creaking and muffled scuffling of Miss Mary's footfalls as she raced up the stairs.

And Grace sat, her foot tap-tapping. The dark seemed too heavy for the candlelight to break through. The quiet hung just as heavy as the smells of musk, soggy wool, ripe peaches, and body odor.

It was all Grace could do to breathe.

"Wade in the water, wade in the water, children. Wade in the water . . . ," Weezy sang, quiet as a cricket's whisper. But in the tiny room, in the dark, it seemed loud enough. There was comfort in the sound. Grace was glad for it.

"Wade in the water, God's gonna trouble the water."

"I know that song," Grace whispered back. "Mamma sings it when she's afraid. She says it's about Moses leading the Israelites out of Egypt, when they come to the Red Sea. Moses told the Israelites to go into the water, have faith, for God would raise up the waters and protect them against the pharaoh's men."

"It's one my pap taught me," said Weezy. "He made us know it by heart for our journey here. Said General Tubman taught it to him. Said when the slave chasers are hunting you down, cross the water and the dogs will lose your scent. The song keeps us safe."

"My mamma is a teacher; she tells us stories." Grace worked hard to swallow her guilt for running away. "She says stories tell us who we are."

"I know another story," Weezy said. "God sent an angel to touch the pool of Bethesda, gave it special powers. And people bathed in them waters, got free of all that ailed them. And here we are, to bathe in them waters of freedom."

"Now you sound like my pappa. When he speaks, his voice is full of sky and trees and swooping barn swallows."

Sorry touched Weezy's shoulder.

"She's no bother, Sorry," Grace said.

"She don't believe it," whispered Weezy. "You free. I heard of free blacks, but I don't believe it neither."

"Now you sound like my mamma. She says there's free for the white, then there's free for the black. Same word, but the word seems smaller for the black folk. But Pappa says there's possibilities. His great-great-grandfather fought in the War of Independence. He was freed when the war was won. We've been free ever since."

"That's why you in this here hidey-hole, because you so free?" Weezy asked.

"Pappa don't walk small for no one," Grace huffed. "Isn't that why you coming up north, to be free?"

"We come up here so not to be killed. Not the same thing."

Loud rapping on the floor above quieted their whispers. Sorry blew out the candle. They heard Mrs. Scott scream, and strange voices boomed in anger, followed by the sound of heavy boots scuffling across the kitchen floor.

Rebels were in the house!

Wade in the water, wade in the water, children. Weezy's song echoed in Grace's thoughts. She closed her eyes tight, and clung to the comfort in the song. *Wade in the water, God's gonna trouble the water.*

She felt Weezy's hand grip hers, and she held it tight.

Then it was quiet, a booming quiet that seemed to last forever. They dared not whisper now, dared not twitch a muscle. And so Grace sat and waited. She waited for Miss Mary. She waited for Pappa.

She waited for the light to find them. *Wade in the water . . .*

More time, more quiet.

She thought of Mamma, and tears of guilt welled up. *Tap-tap-tap* went her foot. She had to hold it to make it stop.

The creaking stairs warned them: someone was coming! Grace couldn't tell if it were a man's step, or a woman's. But whoever it was, they were coming closer. Then someone was scraping against the shutter. Grace held her breath, and her tears rolled. They were found!

Wade in the water . . .

"Gracie?" Miss Mary poked a light into the room. Grace exhaled so hard it hurt. "The rebels are gone. See, we gave them what they wanted, and they left. They were just boys, really. They were far from home, and close to starving, by the looks of them. Gave them a good meal, and they left as they came. But they're coming back."

"They'll come back?" Grace stiffened.

Miss Mary gave a slow nod. "They're coming, they told us. And there's thousands more of them."

PART SEVEN

TILLIE

CHAPTER FIFTEEN

The Same Day: Friday, June 26

The classroom was small and tidy, with a large window facing the streets of Gettysburg. A few had their noses in their readers, but most struggled to see outside. People scattered across the walkways and roads and yards. Her back to the room, Mrs. Eyster was writing on the board, her perfect lettering gliding across the slate without a screech. Tillie was amazed that there was school at all, given the circumstances of the past few days. Most of the colored folk had left, except the stubborn ones like Abraham Bryan. Mother said they should all leave, but Father refused. Many of their neighbors refused, believing the rebs wouldn't get this far north. So they held church services on Sunday, and even opened some shops, and school. Life almost seemed normal.

"The rebels are here!"

"It looks like a big snake."

Tillie rolled her eyes. How many times had they heard those words since Father and the volunteers had gone to fell trees in the Gap to block the rebels' passing? *The rebels are coming!* The call was becoming more like a chicken's chirp. No one believed it anymore.

"The rebels are not coming," Tillie huffed.

"Oh, yes they are." Allison pointed across the town to the seminary. There in the distance, a dense, dark mass moved toward the town.

It *was* like a giant snake, big enough to swallow Gettysburg whole. Tillie's heart pounded. She shook her head in disbelief.

"Ladies." Mrs. Eyster had joined them at the window, herself all atremble. "Hurry home straightaway. Go as quickly as you can!"

Tillie did as she was told. That mass looked too big to be another raiding party sweeping through the town. She had reached York Street when she heard the galloping sounds and shouts of men on horseback. *Rebels!*

At the diamond, she turned onto Baltimore Street and made a beeline home. Looking over her shoulder, she saw nothing behind her. But as she finally reached her own stoop, she could see the rebels nearing her street. Slamming the door behind her, she rushed to the sitting room to find Mother peering out the window.

"They're here, and so many!" Mother stood, pale as a clean sheet. "Where's Father?"

Tillie could hear cavalry racing pell-mell down the road. The very air trembled with the pounding horses hooves and the footfalls of the rebel infantry as they marched through Gettysburg.

"They call themselves human beings?" Tillie looked out the window. "Why, I never saw a more unearthly wild bunch of ruffians—dirty, shoeless, and hatless! What are they going to do, Mother? Are they going to ransack the town again?"

"They won't find much. There's nothing left. Where's Father? Have you seen Father?"

"Why do they do this?"

"Just to frighten us, Tillie." Mother wrung her hands.

"Well," said Tillie, "wait until our boys get them, those dirty scalawags. I have half a mind to—"

"Hush your bold talk, child," Mother scolded her, "and do something useful! Find your father!"

At that moment she heard a fearful screech. Tillie turned to see two rebels leading away her pony! Kicking and screeching in protest, ears flattened against its neck, the pony kicked a rebel. The man shouted, and retaliated with a stick to the pony's neck and forelegs. A third rebel had hold of the Jackson boy by the cuff. Like the pony, the boy kicked and screeched to get away.

"They're taking Sam Jackson!" Tillie screamed, bolting toward the door.

But already Mother was rushing down the stairs and through the door. Tillie ran after her.

"Sir!" Mother pleaded with the soldier. "You don't want that boy. He's too puny, small and lazy, good for nothing. Take the pony, but leave the boy!"

"Not my pony!" Tillie wailed.

Mother cast her an angry look. H*ush!*

"He's your son, ma'am?" The rebel's drawl was thick as fog and hard to understand. But thicker than his drawl was his smell. Tillie winced.

"He helps us out. He's of no use to you," said Mother.

"You are right, ma'am." The rebel let go of Sam Jackson with a heave-ho shake. Sam stumbled under the force. "We don't want the boy. We want the horse."

"But that's just a pony!" Tillie, holding her chin high in defiance, stepped forward.

The soldier chuckled, tipping his hat. He smiled broader, revealing brown, crusted teeth. "We don't want to ride the thing. Horsemeat makes for a good stew!"

Tillie yelled all the louder. "You are a disgrace to humanity, picking on children and pets!" The soldiers walked off, leading the pony. Tillie bit her lip, trying not to cry. But the tears came anyway, and this only fed her anger.

"Beggin' your pardon, ma'am." Both Tillie and Mother swerved to face yet another rebel. Tillie tightened her fist as she took a step forward, but Mother caught her by the arm. The boy standing before them was a pitiful sight. He seemed barely older than Tillie, and his clothes were in tatters and his feet bound in rags. He held his hat with nervous fingers running around the rim. The rifle strapped across his back was as battered as he.

"Would you have food to spare, ma'am?"

"Well," Mother snapped. "Certainly you must ask for something to eat after you bully our children and take our pony!"

"We all do the best we can to get by. It's not fair, ma'am," the soldier said. His drawl, or maybe his hunger, slurred his words. "And it doesn't make sense."

Mother huffed.

To Tillie's shock, she realized Mother meant to feed that creature!

"Come along, boy." Mother led the soldier inside. Tillie refused to be in the same room as the foul little worm. Instead she stood near the door, her eyes narrowed in hate. The rebel gobbled the food as if he hadn't eaten in months. He lacked any trace of civilized manners.

And when he left, she did not return the offered smile, nor accept his stuttering thank-you.

As soon as our boys get here, she thought, *they will put you in your place.*

PART EIGHT

GRACE

CHAPTER SIXTEEN

Saturday, June 27

It was a long, long night.

Grace had stayed in the hidden room, hoping for Pappa to come soon. At long last Miss Mary came and let the three out of the little room. It was hard to move, Grace's legs were so cramped and sore. She blinked, her eyes stinging in the low light. The day before, General Early had demanded a ransom from the town elders: sugar, coffee, bacon, and a thousand shoes. When the mayor refused, saying the town had been stripped to its bones already, the general took his men and set up camp on the eastern slopes of South Mountain. Groups of rebels still made occasional raids through town.

"There is a gathering at the diamond," Miss Mary said as she gave them more food and water, and another candle. "Everyone knows you, Grace, and knows your father. These unsettled times don't bring out the best in people. We have to be careful. The rebels are out there, in plain sight, waiting for reinforcements. The war is coming right here to Gettysburg, as sure as the summer heat."

"What about Pappa?" Grace asked.

"Don't you worry about him," Miss Mary reassured her. "Not too many men are as capable as he."

But Grace couldn't go back into that cellar. She couldn't wait anymore. And she couldn't hold it in anymore, not her guilt or her shame or her worry. She had to do something. She had to do something *now*.

"Miss Mary." Grace stood resolute. "If he can't come fetch me in town, then I have to go to him. I have to go home."

"You can't, Grace. It's too dangerous. The rebels are on South Mountain."

"It's too dangerous for him to come to town because this is where the danger is, not at the farm. Pappa's home, I know it."

"We don't know where he is, Grace."

"Mary." Mrs. Scott stepped up. "Listen to her. It's dangerous for everyone, especially now. For her, and for us."

"I know every way home there is," Grace went on. "I know how to avoid being seen. It won't take but an hour. I won't be seen."

"Grace"—Miss Mary shook her head—"these are strange times, and people will do strange things to get by. And if the rebels catch you, it won't matter who you are. They'll—"

"But they're not *here*." Grace didn't mean to raise her voice as loud as she did, but she wasn't going to take no for an answer. "They moved out, and they won't be back *tonight*. They've gone back to the mountain for reinforcements, that's what you said. Tomorrow will be too late. But tonight it's safe. Tonight, I *have to go home*."

"Mary, listen to her. She's making some sense," Mrs. Scott urged.

"There's no sense to any of this." Miss Mary shook her head, running her fingers through her curls. "There's no sense in you going. But if you stay, and they come back, you may be in worse trouble and I won't be able to protect you. We'll all hang. God help me, what do I do?"

"Pappa will know what happened to Friend Alice," Grace said. "He'll know what to do about Sorry and Weezy."

Miss Mary was still shaking her head when Weezy stepped up. There the two of them stood, Sorry and Weezy.

"We'll go with Grace, Miss Mary," said Weezy. "We can't ask you to put yourself in more danger. Not sure what will happen out there. But here, I do know—them rebs are coming *here*. We may have little chance out there. But we have no chance here."

CHAPTER SEVENTEEN

"You have to look like my sisters, just in case," said Grace, tying the bows. "These are the last dresses in Mr. Scott's store; Miss Mary picked them out, and Mrs. Scott didn't seem very happy about it. Put these clothes on, and no one in town is going to ask us otherwise."

"I ain't never had store clothes before." Weezy brushed the folds of the skirt and fingered the lace trim. "I never seen such fine lace, not even on the mistress. Not sure I like this bonnet, though. And how can anyone work in these gloves? These are just plain silly." Weezy chuckled, hiding it behind her roughened hand.

Sorry stood before the mirror, her trembling fingers tracing the lace tie about her waist. She touched the lace that trimmed the collar, and then touched her cheek and traced her brow. But she said not a word.

All turned their heads as the hall clock struck one in the morning. Miss Mary came into the room. "The streets have quieted. It's now or never, I suppose. God forgive me for letting you go."

"We'll be fine, Miss Mary." Grace shook with the same worry, her feet tap-tap-tapping. She breathed deep and slow. Then, like plunging into a cold creek, she held her breath and led the two sisters through the kitchen door into the alley.

Grace stayed close to the alley's edge, keeping under the drooping overhang of oak and elm. On a clear, quiet day, the trip would take hardly an hour. But now, in the dead of night, they were fugitives, hiding in the moon shadows, and the going was slow. Grace worked her way down the alley. She looked back to Weezy, and motioned for them to stay put. She inched her way along a fence, ducking whenever she heard a noise. Only when she was certain it was safe did she give them a soft, short whistle, *Come along.*

But then she heard voices! Grace stretched her neck around a tree to get a closer listen. She recognized them, and heaved a sigh. They weren't soldiers, they were the neighbors, Mr. Tilimon and his sons. Just like the Scotts and Miss Mary, the Tilimons had decided not to flee the town. And it seemed like they were making a jolly good time of it, too. Grace shook her head; sometimes there was no understanding old people. She crept along, ready to run if need be.

"Who's there?" Mr. Tilimon hooted.

"Who's there?" one of his sons slurred. They had been drinking. Grace knew this made the moment all the more dangerous. Drinking men tended to lose their senses.

"It's just me, Mr. Tilimon," Grace shouted back, disguising her voice. "My sisters and I are helping Miss Mary. One of the babies is sick. We're on our way back now."

"It's mightily late for you to be out and about, don't you think? Soldiers might be out there."

"Glad to see you're safe, too! Babies don't work on anyone's schedule except their own, Mr. Tilimon. With all the commotion these past few days, Miss Mary just thought it best to git while we can."

"Rebels surely did cause a stir. Who did you say you were?"

"It's just me, Mr. Tilimon. I'll tell Miss Mary I saw you. She said she had a meat pie for you, knowing you were feeling poorly of late. She'll be glad to hear you are doing better. Give my best to Mrs. Tilimon!"

Whistling for Weezy and Sorry to follow, she bolted down the alley. She stopped again just before the alley opened up onto Washington Street. A block down the way was the diamond. She motioned for the two to stay put as she moved ahead, looking up and down the road. Behind her, she heard Mrs. Tilimon shouting now at Mr. Tilimon. Mr. Tilimon was shouting back, so loud that a dog barked in complaint. Another man was hooting at all the commotion.

Grace motioned to them, *Hurry on!* At a full run, they crossed the road. Grace hoped no one would pay attention to three more running in the streets, after all the dozens who had fled in the night. She angled off the main road, entering another alley.

Once more she heard voices, and instantly slowed, clinging to the shadows. She motioned Weezy and Sorry to stop, but the two came up, easing next to her.

"Who's there?" someone called out, her voice clear as church bells.

Grace shivered. This one wasn't swooning from too much drink.

"I say, who is there? Come out now!"

"It's just me," Grace said.

"Show yourself, I'm warning you! If I scream, I'm sure to attract lots of attention, and then you'll be in trouble!"

Grace swallowed hard, looking to the runaways, motioning them to stay put. Then she stepped free from the shadows. "It's just me, I tell you. I'm doing an errand for Miss Mary."

"Grace Bryan?" Tillie Pierce stepped forward. "Why would Miss Mary have you out and about at this late hour with rebels so near?" Then Tillie wrenched to a stop, and Grace knew she had seen Weezy and Sorry.

"What are you doing, Grace Bryan?" Tillie whispered hard, her voice trembling. "The rebs will kill us all for sure because of you! I have to turn you in!"

Grace took a step back, but not in fear. "And what are you doing, out and about in the dark by yourself, Miss Tillie? That don't seem like the proper thing to do."

Tillie huffed. "You can't talk to me like that."

"You're not stealing more peaches, are you?" Grace said.

"I was visiting my friend," Tillie huffed. "Not that it's your concern."

Weezy took a slow step forward.

"It's a brave Miss Grace taking us home, miss," she said. "I see you all atremble, and I all atremble. It's not always easy, doing the right thing. Sometimes it too hard to tell the right thing from the proper thing. Sometimes more brave to look past what's proper, and do what's right. Like Job, all them troubles he seen. He was a good man, just like Miss Grace here, just like you, miss. But none of that mattered.

The lord giveth and the lord taketh away, my auntie says. And Job had nothing left. Evil did the best it could to beat Job down, but Job kept true to what's right. He only hoped for the light to show him the way. There's light in your eyes, miss. Please, we just want to go home."

Tillie offered a weak smile. "Well, I can understand, but I can't risk any such dangers to my family. Surely you can see that?" she said.

Grace clenched her fist. There was no time to talk Tillie into agreement. She'd have to take matters into her own hands now.

"Miss Tillie." She stood tall as she could. As Tillie turned around, Grace hit her on the chin, so hard that Tillie spun and fell to the ground.

"Run now!" Grace hissed, taking Weezy's hand.

"Not sure that was the proper or right thing to do." Weezy trembled like she was cold.

"It wasn't," said Grace. "And Mamma will whop me good for it later. But for now, we got to run!"

And they ran, through another alley and another block. She ran as if coals burned hot under her feet. And three lives depended on how fast she could run.

Grace took them out Baltimore Street, and entered Evergreen Cemetery.

"We're almost there." Her chest heaved, her ribs throbbed. Pappa would be angry, but he'd take her in his arms and he'd know what to do about Weezy and Sorry. "Hold there!" a voice shot out in the dark.

No! Grace wheeled, her heart bursting. Not after how far they had come!

"Who are you, there?" the voice thundered again.

"It's just me," Grace replied between heavy breaths.

"Don't play those games with me, child." The figure came closer, his heavy footfalls quickening. The metal of his rifle caught the moonlight and glistened as he lowered it at her.

"Grace Bryan?" Just then the tall figure emerged from the shadows. He clicked his tongue in recognition. "I heard your pappa sent you to Philadelphia."

"The train left without me."

"I doubt that," the man chuckled as he lifted his musket. Grace recognized the chuckle. Mr. Butler. "Good great glory, Grace Bryan. Your pappa is going to bust your hide. And that ain't going to come near what your mamma is going to do."

"Mr. Butler!" Grace cried. "Have you seen Pappa, sir? Have you seen my pappa?"

"He took to the woods before the rebs came. Ain't no one can find Abraham Bryan if he don't want to be found. You, on the other hand, are in a heap of trouble. Who's that with you?"

"Pappa's expecting us home. I best go now."

"Your pappa isn't there, Grace. Earlier today, an advance from the Union army came up the Pike. Your farm is overrun with Union soldiers looking out for the rebel camp. Not too hard to find, if you ask me. There's no more doubt about what's coming here now, Grace Bryan. All the roads come together here in Gettysburg. Next couple of days, the war comes here. You can't go home, Grace."

CHAPTER EIGHTEEN

"Seems like everyone's on the run this night." Mr. Butler led Grace and the girls to the far side of the cemetery, where a wagon was parked, a red flag tied to its seat.

Mr. Butler eased Grace, then Weezy, into the back of the wagon. Sorry waved his arm aside and helped herself. The three lay low in the wagon as he covered them with hay and a blanket. "In a day or two, the town will be overrun with soldiers from both sides. I'm taking you to my sister's house. You can hide out there."

Mr. Butler slapped the reins and the horses neighed. The wagon rolled uneasily over the roughened ground, and lurched to one side. Grace yelped as she rolled into Weezy, who rolled into Sorry. The wagon lurched again as it finally came to the road.

Grace didn't have to see where they were going, for she knew the ground well enough. She felt fear rising in her throat with every wagon bounce. They were heading back to Gettysburg. Back to where they started. She covered her face with her hands.

She couldn't go home. Soldiers had taken over their farm.

Pappa wasn't home.

Grace swallowed her tears, but they grew bigger by the moment, too big to hold down. Just like her fear.

She felt the wagon turn and slow. Finally it stopped. And a moment later, Mrs. Woods flipped the blanket over.

"Negroes, Adam?" Mrs. Woods looked at him with rounded, worried eyes.

"You know Abraham's daughter. He's helped us plenty, now it's our turn to help him."

"If they catch us, Adam, hiding negroes . . ."

"We'll be fine, Sarah." Mr. Butler helped Sorry out of the wagon, while Weezy and Grace jumped free.

Flitting like a bird, Mrs. Woods pushed the girls into the back of the stone house. Grace knew where they were: Culp's Hill. Quickly Mrs. Woods ushered the three into another cellar, into another tiny room.

"You need to be quiet," Mrs. Woods urged. "I'll come down to check on you when I can. Whatever happens, do not make a sound, and do not leave this room!"

The room was smaller than the one in Miss Mary's cellar, no more than a hole in the wall. The slant of the roof made it impossible to sit up. No hay or blankets to cushion them. The three lay on the dirt floor.

"Shame about the dress," Weezy whispered. "It was the best thing I ever hope to have."

Grace nodded.

"Your pappa would be proud of you," Weezy said then.

Grace shook her head. She couldn't speak, worry stealing her voice.

"Grace is a good name," Weezy said. "There's power in a name."

But Grace could only shake her head again.

"Pap says names are our stories. They tell us who we are. They tell us where we come from."

"What kind of name is Weezy?" Grace managed.

"That's just what *they* call me." Weezy chuckled. "My auntie named me Wisdom. Mam's Wisdom, she called me. And you, this is who you are: Abraham was the chosen one, you know, gone on a long journey to the land of milk and honey. He was a peaceable man, and a wise man. God called on him, and Abraham followed. He's the father of faith. And you be Abraham's Grace. Can't be a more powerful name than that."

Grace looked up. A thin ray of moonlight came through a splintered plank and danced across the shiny face of Wisdom.

"That's your name to keep," Wisdom said. "And I'll remember your name, and your story. And wherever we go, I will tell everyone I meet all about Abraham's Grace, who delivered us to safety in the night. And you will remember my name. Wisdom. And you'll tell my story to your pappa, when he comes for you. And you'll tell my story to your mamma when you see her, too. So we won't be forgot. So my mam and my pap won't be forgot. You tell your pappa when you see him?"

"I will tell my pappa," Grace whispered.

She clapped her hands over her mouth, squeezing her eyes shut. Her body shook. Wisdom patted her back, laying her head on her shoulder.

"Yeah, that's what we'll do," she whispered.

PART NINE

ANNIE

CHAPTER NINETEEN

Tuesday, June 30

Annie made her way back to the camp, sore from marching, her arms heavy from the Enfield. And she itched. But as bad as these skeeters were, Dylan was worse, a gnawing itch that just wouldn't let up. He was like James in that, always gnawing away at her. Mama told her to pick her battles, but didn't that Dylan ever give up?

As she stepped closer to the campfire, she saw Dylan had his nose in William's book, and he was tearing a page free of the spine.

And she exploded like buckshot.

"*Enough!*" she shouted, so loud that Gideon stood up at his own campsite. Others, too, looked up with a start. Even as everyone watched, no one moved in their direction.

She lunged into Dylan, so hard that he let loose a grunt as air escaped his lungs. Coughing and sputtering, Dylan dropped to his hands and knees, gripping his chest. Before he moved again, she kicked him, hard enough to spin him over. Before he could gather himself, she puffed herself round and big.

And then she sat right full on top of him, pinning him down with her knees.

"*Dylan, enough with you!*" she boomed, loud as never before, drawing more of a crowd. "I'll whip you easy. Then you'll whip me. Then I'll whip you easy again. Make no mistake, you can't keep me down. I'll always come back and whip you square! You'll not have a moment's rest, for fear of seeing me about to whip you *again*."

"I ain't no coward," Dylan hissed, holding his chest. "I don't give up!"

"No, you ain't a coward," Annie growled back, shaking his shoulder, trying to knock the sense into him. "You sticking up for that family in town proves that. But I ain't no coward either. Seems to me, we're more alike than different. Let's leave it at that."

She raised herself slowly off Dylan, who lay as still as death more from the force of her voice than from her weight. She picked up her brother's book, brushing the dirt and mud from its cover.

Gideon's voice was deep and low like a preacher's, scolding. "You two at it again? Didn't you get enough of that in town? Maybe some extra chores might help calm your spirits."

Annie tied her handkerchief tight about her mouth and nose, and shoved her hands into her leather gloves. She grabbed a shovel and moved toward the company "sink." The latrine.

"Pop?" Dylan shouted out in a final plea. Gideon raised his arm, dismissing the young soldier as he walked back to the tents. Dylan grunted, turning toward the job at hand.

Annie chuckled. But her smile quickly vanished as her boots sank ankle deep into the muck, making a gurgly sound as she lifted them.

Dylan wheezed, turning as green as the waters pooling about them. Then he sputtered, spitting as he tasted the air, driving his shovel into the muck not far from her, glaring at her. But neither opened his mouth to talk, especially as the sun rose higher, heating the day.

It was a hopeless cause to clean out the long, open ditches. The more they worked to bury the muck, or at least move it away from their tents, the more it oozed. The slick of slime crept across the ground. The smell was powerful and raw, the air thick with flies. Black gnats swarmed the back of her neck and ears, and itched as fierce as the heat, under her arms, behind her knees, even in her ears. She'd risk another cigar, if need be, to be rid of these nippers.

"Blasted gallinippers," she yelped.

"Bloody damn hell," Dylan wheezed, swatting at the flying cloud, leaning against the shovel. "Them's not just any nippers. Them's graybacks for sure. Only one way to get rid of them; you'll have to shake your duds over the fire. They jump like regular popping corn."

Annie scowled, shaking her head.

"You think you got something nobody else does?" Dylan swung his shovel. "Can't be shy in the army, strawfoot!"

Evening couldn't come fast enough. Finally Jasper came to fetch them, with orders to wash before coming to camp. Before Jasper could finish his sentence releasing them from duty, Annie dropped her shovel and raced off. She had been careful since the first day to stay private about her routines. She recognized early on that taking no baths encouraged others to keep their distance. But now she'd risk the chance. There wasn't a place on her that didn't itch fierce as fire.

And she didn't slow any as she reached the pond. She jumped—boots, clothes, and all. The itching burned right through her, a thousand needling buggers all feeding on every inch of her body. She peeled off her britches, throwing them ashore, and scrubbed with pond sand until she was near raw. Taking off her shirt, she scrubbed with the same fierceness. Again and again she plunged, until at last the itching eased to tolerable. Her head just barely above the water, she let the pond's coolness ease her soreness.

Good great glory. She moaned and shook her head, remembering how carefully she had carried her boots across the Potomac. Now they were covered in muck.

"Hey, strawfoot!" a voice called from the woods.

"Jiggers," another chuckled.

Annie stayed nose deep in the water. Little moonlight filtered through the tree cover, but she could see the long shadow stretching across the shore. Dylan and Jasper!

"So, strawfoot, come and get your britches!"

CHAPTER TWENTY

She was done for!

Annie stayed put, stirring the water very little. She couldn't go deep enough, or far away enough, to hide. If Dylan took another step, he'd see her in all her glory.

"Privates!" another voice boomed in the distance, and all three—Dylan and Jasper on the pond's edge, and Annie in the water—snapped to as a soldier stepped into the moonlight. "Haven't learnt your lesson yet? You two get back to camp now. Step lively. Gideon wants you *yesterday*. And you in the water"—he threw Annie her britches—"move it quick!"

"Yes, sir!" Annie boomed, slipping into her pants.

The soldier stepped back into the shadows, stomping through the woods in a hasty retreat. Annie climbed out of the water, wringing her shirt dry and shaking out her boots.

As she entered the camp, she found Dylan and Jasper crouched before the fire in front of the tent.

"How's them woods, strawfoot?" Still smelling like latrine sweat, Dylan smirked, winking at Jasper.

Gideon spat. He eased next to the fire, tapping his pipe, and the skirmish was over.

Others of the Ninth walked into the camp, too, sitting between Dylan and Annie, crowding around the fire, aiming to keep the peace.

"I, for one, am spoiling for a good fight," one spoke up. "Them

Federals are a bunch of thieves with no regard for personal rights. We've been putting those blue-belly cowards in their place all along. Let's finish the job so we can go home."

"Hear! Hear!" rose a cheer.

"Heard tell they bayonet the prisoners of war, slash their throats, and cut their tongues out. Uncivilized they are, just plain scum."

"We can always have James here sit on them," Gideon said then, lighting his pipe. "It seems to do the trick."

Chuckles rumbled through the crowd. Even Dylan had to crack his crooked grin, still rubbing his chest. Annie smiled, too, turning and smoothing the pages of William's book.

"Sergeant?" Jasper spoke up. "What was the fiercest battle you ever saw?"

Gideon puffed more circles as he searched his memory. He had seen the battle between the ironclads, the USS *Monitor* and the CSS *Virginia*. He had seen his home city, Portsmouth, burned to the ground by the Federals. He had fought in the battle of Seven Pines and in the Seven Days Campaign, where the company fought courageously at Malvern Hill. There wasn't too much he hadn't seen.

"Boys"—he lit his pipe slowly, and drew a breath—"there was one particularly gruesome fight. A group of us had gone foraging one warm night and came to rest on the banks of a river. Now just so happens, across the very same river camped a bunch of blue boys. And by and by they noticed us. 'How's old Jeff?' one called out. 'Come to Richmond and see for yourself,' I yelled back. 'Enough with the jawing,' he shouted back. And we knew the battle was begun. Then, by thunder, this Federal took to singing a round of "Yankee Doodle." Not to be outdone, we sang two rounds of "Dixie." They opened fire with "Hail, Columbia," and we fired back with "Bonnie Blue Flag." Then it was all quiet. We thought we won this battle. Then a voice rang out, the purest voice I ever heard."

And then the burly Gideon sang, his voice rising in an unexpected tenor. A moment later, Jasper joined in perfect harmony, his voice that of an angel.

We're tenting tonight on the old campground.
Give us a song to cheer
Our weary hearts, a song of home,
And friends we love so dear. . . .

When the song was over, Gideon hit his pipe on a rock to clean its bowl. "That voice shot us all down that night, brought us all to tears. That voice raised us above the war, made us men again. I tell you, it was a brutal and bloody battle, ripping our very hearts out."

As Annie looked around, she saw as many casualties here, their faces shadowed in the moonlight.

"Boy"—Dylan broke the silence, turning to Jasper—"once your voice changes, you'll sound full-growed."

"Jiggers," Jasper said then. "Your voice changed, and you still sound like a pig's fart."

The men of the Ninth crowed with laughter. Even Annie had to laugh. Dylan gave a nod to Gideon, who smiled and winked at his boy.

"What are you going to do after the war, sergeant?" Jasper said then.

"I suppose I'll pick up the plow again."

Dylan whistled. "I hope not, Pop. Picking up the plow is one thing. Making it work is another."

Gideon chuckled. "Naw, I suppose I won't. Your ma could, though. She could make anything work." He smiled at his son, and tousled his hair. He turned to Annie. "And you, James Anachie Gordon, what plans do you carry with you?"

"I want to go out west," Annie said. "They say, out west all things are possible."

Jasper smiled large as his feet. "Hear tell there's so much land out west, they don't know what to do with it all. River water so sweet, bees drink it. The land so rich, wheat and corn grow six feet overnight. Jiggers! A garden of Eden, hear tell."

"Seems the only place possible for a big foot like you!" Annie said flatly. The soldiers hooted in merriment, including Jasper himself.

"Why not home, strawfoot?" Dylan asked.

Annie shrugged. "I've no home left to return to. The Yanks burned most of the farm. The war took my brothers. My pap died, and my mama left to live with her sister. And I didn't leave on good terms with my mama. Don't know if she'll want me back."

Gideon leaned back. "Whatever was done then, can't see that it matters now. I know it wouldn't matter to me so long as everyone got home."

Dylan gave a nod, and looked at his pop.

"We'll go out west, you and me, James!" Jasper hooted. "Besides, I hear tell those western ladies are filled with sass and gumption. What say you, James, the two of us out west!"

"Well"—Annie gave a slow nod—"I'm quite fond of gumption."

Then someone began a tune on his harmonica, a rowdy tune that spurred another to join in with a foot-stomping fiddle.

And as the men sang, Gideon leaned in close to Annie.

"Need to ask you a favor, son," he said, his voice low and solemn as a grave. "I've been long gone from home. I was never a good farmer, but I was good enough for my wife and my sons. Not been a man of church, leastways not to my wife's thinking. But I always tried to do right by them. I need you to do me a favor, James Anachie Gordon. I need you to write me a letter, just in case. They should have some words to remember me by."

Annie understood: they were going into battle soon, and it was going to be a fierce one.

Annie nodded.

"Thank you mightily, son," Gideon said. "I'll get the paper and whatever else you need. I am not without my resources." He pouched his pipe.

That night, as she rolled onto her blanket under a sky heavy with stars, she saw that the Whitworth lay by her haversack pillow. It had been cleaned bright as ever. Near to it was her box of cartridges.

Seems like done is done, Annie thought.

PART TEN

THE FIRST DAY

Wednesday, July 1

CHAPTER TWENTY-ONE

TILLIE

"I did not raise a ruffian! Out at such an hour, when no proper lady would dare venture!" Mother wailed in utter horror. "What would the neighbors think!"

"Well, not too many neighbors left to think one way or the other," said Father from behind the newspaper. Tillie could almost hear him grin. "Did you at least get a good swipe in?"

"Father!" Mother swerved about, all the more horrified.

"I was gathering flowers, Mother," Tillie explained again. "I just wanted some flowers from the neighbor's garden just across the way, in case our boys came by, and I fell in the alley. Let the neighbors talk, I say. Seems to me there are more important matters to talk about than what one silly girl does."

Father flipped the newspaper page down, looking at her, startled. "Such wise words coming from *my* little girl?"

Mother cleared her throat. "It's just dangerous out there. You never know who's watching, child."

"I know, Mother. Sometimes, though, one has to do the right thing, even if it's not necessarily the proper one."

Father once again peeked over the newspaper, and this time she could see his grin. "Who are you and what did you do with my silly daughter?" He winked at her, and Tillie smiled.

With the arrival of General Buford's Union cavalry the day before, settling on the outskirts east of town, Union soldiers swept the area for any lingering rebel forces. They found them. Musket fire crackled on the western ridge as the two forces met. The Union force clashed with the rebels on Chambersburg Pike along Seminary Ridge. All morning, blue uniforms filed through Gettysburg, heading toward the booming fire of artillery.

Tillie waved a hearty welcome to the soldiers. Such a dashing sight! A few trickles of townsfolk also came out of hiding onto the streets, offering water and milk, pies and bread. And Tillie gave them flowers. She saw the Tilimons, and the Scotts. And Miss Mary. Her teacher, too. It was as if the town let loose a collective sigh of relief: *at long last, we are safe.*

For hours, everyone stood in the heat, cheering their noble boys on.

As noon approached and the parade moved on, townsfolk lingered on the streets, but Tillie dashed home.

"They were smartly handsome, Mother!" Tillie hooted. "And I tell you, they were very reassuring. They'll send those rebel traitors back to the southland!"

"Tillie!" Her mother shook her head. Father was still outside, talking to neighbors and watching the troops, trying to gather information. Someone tapped on the door.

"Please forgive the intrusion." Their neighbor Henrietta Schriver gave a nervous smile. She was no taller than a minute, and the whole of her trembled. "They're bringing the wounded into town."

Tillie looked to Mother.

"Whose wounded, Henrietta?" Mother asked. "What are you saying?"

"Everyone, from both armies. They've filled the seminary on the ridge with wounded, and the churches on the west side. There's so, so many that now they're bringing them into our homes. The battle is going to sweep right through our town. I don't feel safe here anymore. I want to go to my father's farm." She spoke so fast, she seemed out of breath.

"I thought we'd be safe here." Mother offered the poor woman a cup of tea. "Father said that both armies have a rule they follow: not to harm the civilians."

"Margaret, except for my little ones, all my family are at the farm. I want to be with them now. I just came by to see if you'd like to join me. We'll be safe at the farm."

Mother looked to Father, then to Tillie. "Father won't leave, and I'm not leaving him. But please take Tillie with you. She can help you with the children."

"No, Mother." Tillie shook her head. "I don't want to leave you."

"This isn't a request, Tillie." Mother smiled. "I need to know you'll be safe."

"I'll be just a moment, then," Tillie huffed, stomping upstairs to her room.

"Tillie!" Mother called after her. "How many times do I have to tell you, ladies don't stomp!"

Tillie gathered her shawl and a bonnet. Then she spied her new dress and petticoats. She had been working on them for a whole year, the petticoats with the eyelet lace, and the skirt with its perfect roses. She could still finish them at the farm. She wrapped them in a bundle and raced downstairs, slowing to a walk as she entered the kitchen.

Hugging her mother, and strapping her bundle about her waist, she followed Henrietta out the door. In tow were Henrietta's two children, Sarah and Mary, both full of tears and wiggles. Taking Sarah's hand, Tillie followed Henrietta as they walked quickly up Baltimore Street, weaving past small groups of Union soldiers, and across the road into Evergreen Cemetery.

"It's not far now." She tugged at Sarah's hand. "It's just on the other side of that rise!"

"Quickly now!" Henrietta called over her shoulder.

Union soldiers walked through the cemetery, laying down many of the more ornate tombstones. It looked like angels lying on the ground, so many had been toppled. Another soldier was setting up a cannon.

"You're destroying our cemetery?" Henrietta cried out. "Is nothing sacred to you?"

"Sorry, ma'am." The soldier tipped his hat, staring at his feet. "We were just trying to save them, just in case there's fighting."

"Fighting?" Henrietta shot Tillie a frightened look. Tillie's heart drummed with dread. "So close to town? When?"

"You shouldn't be here, ma'am." Another soldier approached Henrietta. He tipped his hat, then pointed to the cannon behind them. "Sharpshooters have been picking off our boys as they walk. As soon as they spot the cannon, the rebs will start shelling this whole area."

Henrietta started off, Tillie following close at her heels. They moved over the rise, reaching Taneytown Road, where they were met by a rush of traffic: men and horses and wagons crowded the way. This was not the orderly formation of the day before, with the soldiers marching in tidy columns up the Pike and through the town. This was chaos, men running this way and that way. Some were headed toward the battle on the ridge, looking as weary as those returning from it.

And those returning seemed barely able to walk. Heads and arms bandaged, they carried others on litters or over their shoulders.

At that moment a wagon careened by, spraying everyone with dust and pebbles.

"It's General Reynolds!" the wagon driver shouted. "He's dead! He's dead!"

"Let's hurry," Tillie told Henrietta, but the words scratched her throat. Henrietta nodded, looking up the road, where her family's farm waited, then down the road, back to Gettysburg. Tillie did her best to soothe Sarah, but the girl was crying uncontrollably, reaching for her mother.

"Ma'am?" a young soldier stepped from the archway. "You shouldn't be here. It's not safe."

"So we've been told." Henrietta was near to tears. "I'm trying to get to my father's house, on the east side of the Round Tops."

"It seems no matter where we go, we run into new danger," said Tillie.

"We must hurry." The soldier took Henrietta's arm. "I've stopped a wagon and persuaded the driver to take you as passengers."

Tillie grimaced. The wagon carried wounded soldiers, their clothes ragged and bloody, with bandages that did little to cover their wounds. They moved—as much as they could—to make room for them. But when the soldier lifted Mary and Sarah into the back of the wagon, the wounded seemed to come to life. They smiled and winked and waved and cooed. The children giggled in reply, which made some of the soldiers weep.

The wagon's wheels jostled along the ruts. The horses struggled to pull the wagon forward, neighing and heaving. Tillie clung tight to the side, as the jostling shook her bones and rattled her teeth. Behind her, soldiers moaned in misery. She held her breath against the dust and the heat. But there was no cutting off the smell and taste of blood.

Then they passed the Bryan house.

Tillie gasped. Most of the famous peach orchard had been cut to stumps. Oh, to see it in ruins! The apple orchards were gone. The fields had been stomped flat. The gardens had been picked clean to dust. There were more men than blades of grass, standing everywhere.

Tillie closed her eyes, her stomach wrenching. Grace and the runaways. *They'd been heading here. They didn't make it.*

Poor Grace Bryan.

Finally the wagon reached the farm of Henrietta's father, Jacob Weikert. The big stone house stood in the shadow of the Round Tops. Tillie could hear the popping of gunfire in the distance.

She looked back toward town. She'd be safe, she thought, surrounded by the Union camp. But what of Mother and Father?

Sarah and Mary jumped down and ran to their grandfather. Soldiers helped Henrietta off the wagon, but Tillie jumped, anxious to feel solid earth under her feet.

The wagoner tipped his hat and slapped the reins. The horses neighed. The soldiers waved good-bye. The wagon was swallowed in the tide as another column of men, horses, wagons, and artillery made its way down the road.

PART ELEVEN

THE
SECOND
DAY

Thursday, July 2

CHAPTER TWENTY-TWO

ANNIE

At three in the morning, a time when even ghosts slept, they finally got their orders. They were marching east. Lee was determined to meet the enemy at Gettysburg.

"This is it." Dylan spat as he emerged from the tent, looking at Annie. "The games are done. Now you'll show your grit for true."

Annie nodded.

Tents were being pulled down, rolled up, and packed into wagons with the mess box and kettles. Mules and horses were fed, harnessed, and saddled. Annie packed her knapsack: three days of rations, close to forty rounds of ammunition for the Whitworth, her haversack, and her brother's book.

"You should toss that book of yours," Dylan said. "It'll get heavy on the road. Stow that fancy rifle in the mess wagon. It won't do you any good where we're going. The cook will keep it safe, I promise."

"I'll throw the Enfield away before my gun or my book." They were all she had of home. She strapped the Whitworth to her back.

At that moment Jasper came up from behind, his mouth so full he could barely chew.

"What are you doing? Eating your rations all up in one meal?" Dylan chuckled.

"Seems to me, it's lighter to carry it in my gullet than on my back." Jasper swallowed.

Dylan laughed, slapping Jasper on the shoulder.

"Fall in!" Gideon boomed. Down the line, other sergeants echoed the call to their men.

Annie went to the left of the line and found her place in the middle of the last row, with Dylan flanking her on one side and Jasper on the other.

"Count off!" Gideon barked, and roll call was taken.

The night was hot enough, promising a day right out of hellfire. Annie drank up the night air, knowing that once dawn broke, the breeze would die.

There the column stood, waiting, waiting, waiting. Thousands of restless feet shuffled, hundreds of horses neighed and stomped, mules brayed impatiently.

"Bloody hell," Dylan wheezed. "Hurry up and wait, that's the way of it." *Waiting, waiting, waiting . . .*

Finally the call to march echoed down the line. But even then, another hour passed before the bugle rent the air. The column was creaking to a slow start, but it was moving forward. Thousands of feet pounded the hardened road to the beat of thousands of tin cups banging against thousands of canteens. As the column moved, it rolled like thunder across the mountainside.

Gettysburg was a long day's march away, twenty-five miles through the South Mountains by way of Cashtown Gap.

Tramp, tramp, tramp. One foot in front of the other.

The eastern sky pinked as day broke. The breeze died away, leaving the air hot and humid.

"Ain't it a grand sight, strawfoot?" Dylan smiled, looking ahead of him. "Like a bull snake gliding through the waters!"

Ahead of them, the column of men stretched as far as forever. The cavalry led the way, with the infantry following, then the artillery.

Tramp, tramp, tramp. She marched without tripping, without misstepping, without thinking.

Tramp, tramp, tramp. The sun rose higher. Even the swarms of nippers and gnats fled the heat. The dust cloud rose under Annie's feet and clung to the sweat dripping on her face. The sweat under her arms rolled down her sides and back. The strap holding the Whitworth cut into her shoulder. Annie's throat was parched so dry, it hurt to breathe.

Down the line, canteens flashed as soldiers bottomed up.

Jasper groaned.

"Seems like your big plan is about to backfire," Annie said.

Jasper started to guzzle water, but Dylan pulled the canteen away.

"Sip lightly," he warned. "Too much of a good thing will give you the heave-ho."

Dylan pulled up some grass, wetting it with water and stuffing it under Jasper's hat. Annie was surprised, as surprised as when she had first seen the dandified lawyer smile. Dylan showing worry for someone else seemed as odd as a skunk without stripes.

The sun kept trudging upward and the column kept moving onward. Jasper staggered in the heat, fumbling with his rifle. But he kept marching.

Then someone ahead shouted, "Water!" The call flowed down the ranks like a fast wind. Soldiers broke formation, rushing to the pond.

"Stay where you are, boys," Gideon boomed in warning. "We'll be down for a rest soon enough. Don't break ranks!"

And nobody did, not from the Ninth.

Tramp, tramp, tramp.

Suddenly Jasper groaned again, clutching his gut.

"And thar she blows," Dylan said as Jasper stepped from the column, hunching over on the roadside, heaving his rations.

The road narrowed. The column marched only four men shoulder to shoulder, sometimes only two abreast. But on they marched. *Tramp, tramp, tramp.*

Weary soldiers crowded the roadside. Some sat, heads sagging between their legs. Others lay sprawled where they fell. Soldiers behind them stepped over the fallen, and on they marched. *Tramp, tramp, tramp.*

But the boys of the Ninth stayed in ranks.

The sun rose higher. Annie looked up, catching a glint of metal in the distance. She knew that sparkle.

"Sergeant!" She pointed. "Rifles!"

She heard the crack of rifle fire. Ahead, a man was knocked backward off his horse as the sniper's bullet found its mark. The riderless horse raced down the line in wild-eyed panic.

"Bushwackers! Watch the rocks, sons!" Gideon shouted.

Another bullet zinged so close, she thought for sure she felt its wind. Just two rows ahead, another man fell.

Cavalry raced up and down, getting their own shots off.

But not even the bushwackers could slow their march. *Tramp, tramp, tramp.*

Jasper groaned again. His legs wobbled and his hands trembled, as if the heat had melted them. He tripped. Down he fell, tagging Dylan and Annie as he did so.

A lieutenant on horseback rode up to the fallen Jasper.

"Get up, soldier! Get up or you'll be shot for desertion!"

But all Jasper could do was shake his head and moan, "Jiggers."

Breaking ranks, Dylan jumped the two strides to reach Jasper, and hoisted him to his feet. Surprising herself, Annie also left the line, looping Jasper's dangling arm about her shoulders. Dylan grinned. Together, Dylan and Annie moved Jasper forward. The lieutenant made a move to say something, when Gideon stepped forward, placing himself between his boys and the lieutenant, and snapped a perfect salute.

"Begging your pardon, sir. Isn't it about that time, sir?"

"About what time, sergeant?"

"Break time, sir. Haven't had one in an hour or so."

The lieutenant looked to the sergeant, then to the boys. And Jasper groaned.

"My boys here were just taking this fellow to the wagon, weren't you, boys? They'll be double-quick about it!" Gideon glanced back at Dylan and Annie. "Time to be hoofin' it, boys."

"Yes, sir!" Dylan and Annie shouted.

Dylan and Annie took Jasper to the nearest wagon. It wasn't a far walk, since they were already near the end of the column. The wagon continued to rumble on as Dylan and Annie heaved Jasper onto it.

"Rest easy, chum!" Dylan said.

Jasper moaned. "Can't be killing no blueberries without me!"

"You mean blue-bellies?" Annie smiled.

Jasper slumped in a dead faint.

Tamp, tramp, tramp. The line followed Old Chambersburg Pike, rising past apple orchards and open fields, moving toward the wooded slope of Cashtown Gap. As the sun reached its peak, the day's heat climbed to boiling. More soldiers fell by the wayside. By noon they had reached the Gap.

Suddenly, soldiers ahead raised a howl, and the shouting worked its way down the line like ripples in a pond.

A rider flew past them, shouting: "They've been fighting at Gettysburg! Since yesterday morning! We're driving the blue-bellies back! We've got six thousand prisoners! Huzzah Lee!"

The men shouted: "Huzzah! Lee!"

Even the fallen rallied and stood to join the line. The column pushed on, and the men now sang:

> *Then I wish I was in Dixie!*
> *Hurray! Hurray!*
> *In Dixie's land I'll take my stand,*
> *To live and die in Dixie!*

Not even the clouds of dust could stifle their singing. As tired as they were, their spirits soared as high as the notes. They had courage and dash, and they were going to give the Federals a good taste of both!

Tramp, tramp, tramp.

It didn't take long for the heat to snatch away their voices. The pace, already slow, became tortured. Annie hardly felt the itch from the skeeters anymore. She hardly felt anything.

Tramp, tramp, tramp.

In the distance, in that little town of Gettysburg, the artillery boomed. At last, at four in the afternoon, the bugle sounded the fall-out. The troops scattered to the roadside and swarmed the creeks.

Annie, the sweat pouring from her, drank deep from a creek. Then she eased against the trunk of a tree, knapsack and rifle still on her back, and hung her head.

Already she was asleep.

CHAPTER TWENTY-THREE

TILLIE

Grandfather Weikert welcomed them kindly, and Grandmother Weikert's arms opened wide enough to embrace everyone at once.

Tillie let loose a heavy sigh of relief after leaving the wagon. But even before she had a chance to inhale, more Union forces moved past the farm, racing toward the battle on the western side of town. In the hours since they had began their trek out of town, the battle had moved south, erupting in skirmishes all along the ridge. The Northern army occupied the high ground from Culp's Hill right down the spine of Cemetery Ridge, where Tillie and Henrietta had walked.

The Southern army was spreading along Seminary Ridge, right down to Rose Woods, Stony Hill . . . and the Round Tops.

And just as the soldier from the cemetery gatehouse had predicted, the rebels began firing their cannons at the cemetery. Even where Tillie stood, two miles down the road, she could hear the earth exploding around the gatehouse and along the road.

The explosions were getting closer, louder.

Tillie realized in dread, the war had followed them to the farm! They were surrounded!

Suddenly the field next to the stone house exploded fom the impact of a shell. A man flew backward high into the air. He came down with a thud, landing so close that Tillie could see that his eyes had been blown out of his face. His clothes and skin were blackened by fire. The man gasped as others quickly came to his aid. Lifting him gently, they brought him into the house.

Behind them, a group of soldiers rushed past the house, pursuing the rebs who'd fired the cannon.

Tillie turned as another line of soldiers shouted, swarming the spring close to the house. Like bees in a flower patch, the men drank deep and fast. An officer rode up, shouting for them to fall back into formation. The men turned, dragging their feet, begrudging the order but following it all the same.

"Tillie!" Henrietta shouted, running up behind her. "Come along, Tillie! Take these buckets. I've tin cups from the kitchen. Fill the buckets with spring water, take them to the road!"

Still wearing her bundle, Tillie filled a bucket at the spring and dragged it along, spilling most of the water on the ground, soaking her dress and her bundle. She filled it again, and dragged it to the road. She offered cup after cup to the thirsty soldiers. Soon enough the bucket was empty.

"Get another bucket, Tillie!" Henrietta urged her.

Back and forth she trudged, to the spring then to the road. Her arms hurt so, she thought they'd fall off. Blisters bubbled on her palms, and then burst, leaving open sores that burned like fire. Through the day and well into the early evening, Grandmother Weikert brought bread to Henrietta and Tillie to give to the soldiers.

And when the spring was dry, Henrietta moved Tillie to the pump on the south side of the house.

"Excuse me, miss?" Three officers had ridden up. One young officer dismounted and approached her. "That water looks mighty fine."

"You'll excuse the tin cup," Tillie said. At another time she might have smiled, she might have thought him dashing and noble. But now she was tired beyond thought and reason. Her fingers trembled; it was all she could do to hold the cup.

The soldier swallowed the water slowly, and when he finished, he let loose a sigh so deep it seemed to rise up from his soul. "I can say with all honesty that never have I tasted such sweet water as this!" He smiled.

At that moment the tide of men and wagons on the road shifted to one side, like a creek making a sudden turn. Several officers on horseback rode past them. The man in the center seemed to ride taller than the others. All around, cheers boomed as loud as cannon fire.

"Who is that?" Tillie asked.

"Why, that's General Meade. He's the best hope for the Union, now that General Reynolds is gone. He's going to push that troublesome Lee all the way back to Richmond. Don't you worry none. All this will soon pass, and we'll be well gone." Offering Tillie a quick bow, the soldier leapt onto his horse and rode after the procession. She wondered when the horses might drink.

As the sky glowed with twilight, Tillie continued to give water and bread to passing soldiers. They kept coming, thousands of them, it seemed. Only when her arms hurt so much she thought they'd fall off did she finally go into the house. But nothing hurt as much as her heart. She worried for Father and Mother. She slumped in a chair, rubbing salve into her palms.

Suddenly, a soldier pushed open the front door. He held his hand up to reveal his thumb, bone exposed, flesh hanging on by a thread.

"That looks dreadful!" Tillie exclaimed. Henrietta and Grandmother Weikert hurried into the room, followed by Grandfather Weikert.

The soldier pointed behind him. "More are coming."

Two more soldiers hobbled in, one with his arm in a sling and the other with his head bandaged. More came, spilling into the parlor and the side rooms, and then filling the bedrooms. Like floodwaters rising, there seemed no end to them.

Tillie set to work, tearing sheets into bandages until her fingers were numb and her blisters broke open and bled.

"I can't stay here another moment," Tillie cried. "I just can't!" She dashed out the door, down the short path to the barn. Opening the barn door, she reeled from the smell.

Everywhere they lay, moaning, groaning, bleeding, dying. So many and so close to each other that the hay-strewn floor had disappeared. The sounds of the wounded cut deeper than any blister on her hand.

"Miss?"

Tillie swerved to face a dark-eyed, dark-haired nurse looking up from his charge. She couldn't stop shivering, and her shivering shook her tears loose.

"Miss?" the nurse approached her. "Are you hurt, miss?"

She couldn't stop trembling, not even to shake her head no. Instead, she turned and ran back to the house. But there was no place to go to get away from the smells and the sounds and the sights of the dying, the boys dirty and tattered and broken. They weren't noble or handsome anymore. Some no longer looked human, so shattered were they.

It was Grandmother Weikert who found her standing in the corner.

"This is terrible, indeed." Grandmother wrapped her in a big hug, just as Mother used to do. "And no child should ever have to witness such a horror. But Tillie, hold your tears and your fears. Be brave for now."

Tillie swallowed. "I didn't think it would be like this."

"Don't think, not now. Make yourself some tea. Tea is good for the nerves. Take a breath, Tillie dear. We'll do what we can for them now. We'll deal with our tears later."

Tillie gave a slow nod.

Dawn broke, bright and clear. Tillie didn't know when she fell asleep, or even that she had, until she woke up. Her arms still ached and her palms burned.

Like a waking nightmare, there came the sounds of more marching soldiers. She hurried outside to see regiment after regiment heading down the road toward town. The fields to the east and all along Cemetery Hill were filled with troops. Officers on horseback galloped up and down the long lines of soldiers and tents.

"I've been sitting here most of the night, watching them dig in." Grandfather Weikert shook his head, stroking his chin as he stared across the field.

"I thought it would be safe here." Henrietta shook her head. "Tillie, I'm so sorry."

"Henrietta." Grandfather Weikert's eyes narrowed with worry. "Gather what you need. There's that old farm a half mile across the fields to the east. Take the children and go. You'll be safe there."

"What about you, Papa?"

"I'm staying to keep an eye on things here."

Quickly Tillie and Henrietta, Mary, and Sarah made ready to flee. Grandmother Weikert refused to leave her husband behind, and waved them on. But they didn't get far before a soldier stopped them.

"Fightin's begun on the Round Tops," the soldier told them. "Your house is tucked in close to the rocky ledge. The shells will just pass over your house. But that farmhouse you're headin' for is already a goner! You're better off to stay put."

That very moment, a shell whistled above their heads. The soldier lunged to the ground, taking Sarah with him. Sarah screeched as loud as the shell.

Henrietta dropped, pulling Mary close to the ground with them. Tillie dropped, too, and buried her nose in the dirt, cupping her hands over her ears. The earth trembled as the shell exploded. She couldn't breathe. Her lungs twisted inside her.

"Go back!" the soldier shouted, helping Henrietta to her feet. Tillie coughed dirt and dug more dirt from her ears and nose. More shells screamed over their heads. Tillie looked up to see a bright glow hanging above the town.

"There!" she screamed. "Is the town on fire?"

Henrietta pulled her along.

"Papa!" Henrietta shrieked as she ran back to the stone house. "Gettysburg is on fire!"

"No, no." Grandfather Weikert met them. "The town is fine. But I was wrong, Henrietta. The rebels are on *this* side of the Round Tops, and they're moving in. I should never have sent you away. I don't know what to do anymore." He pointed to the men in gray moving toward Taneytown Road.

Tillie swerved at the sound of fife and drum, announcing the Pennsylvania Reserves! She wanted to shout hooray! These were her friends. Her brothers were marching with them. She cried in relief. They marched double-quick, moving between the barn and the Round Tops, firing as they ran. The rebels barely got a shot off, retreating as quickly as they had come.

More shattered and dying soldiers now filled the yard around the house and the orchard just beyond. The dark-eyed, dark-haired nurse rushed by, taking hold of Tillie's arm. He had emerged from the house carrying a bundle of clothes—her bundle of clothes.

He was panting. "These are all I could find. Someone's treasures, to be sure, but now I need them for a greater cause. Could you tear them up for bandages, miss?"

"I'm sure the owner of these clothes would agree." Tillie took a deep breath. Was it only yesterday she thought them so precious? She tore the petticoats with the eyelet lace, making sure the strips were wide enough for a proper bandage. She tore the skirt with its perfect roses. And when she had finished, she draped the strips across her arm and went to the barn.

"Miss!" The nurse waved at her. "I need your help now."

Next to the nurse stood the man blinded and burned. His eyes now wrapped in linen, he had taken to his feet in fevered panic, feeling his way along the wall. Quickly the nurse led the wounded man to his bed on the floor. Then he turned to Tillie, ushering her to another patient.

"Hold this man's arm, here!" the nurse said. The soldier's shirt was ripped and bloody. His arm was shredded to the bone. As she gripped his arm, the soldier screamed.

"Hold it tighter, miss," the nurse said. Tillie pressed down, and the wounded soldier screamed again. Quickly the nurse wrapped the man's arm. "You're doing good, miss. Just keep holding. The doc has his hands full." The nurse wagged his head toward the other side of the barn. There, under lantern light, a doctor operated on a wounded man held down on the table by three soldiers. The man screamed a long, ragged scream as the doctor sawed.

Tillie felt her lungs squeeze again.

As the nurse finished the soldier's arm, he moved on to the next man. Tillie shadowed him, handing him more bandages as he asked.

When the strips ran out, she looked down, squeezing the folds of her dress. Blood had dried on the calico, but the petticoat was clean enough. She tore at the hem of her petticoat.

"Thank you for your help, miss." The nurse finally looked up.

"For modesty's sake, that's the end of bandages." Tillie tried to smile, but the nurse ran off to his next patient. Tillie stood alone in a sea of bodies. She trembled all over, tears welling up so fast her eyes hurt.

To be here. She shook her head. *In such a terrible place.*

"Miss?" a voice called out. She turned to see a man lying on the floor behind her. His arm was bandaged to the shoulder, more linen wrapping his chest. The linen was already soaked with his blood. She stooped next to him, her fingers gently untying the bandage. Quickly she cleaned the wound. The man winced, but he didn't yelp. His smile was steadfast. Tearing another strip away from her petticoat, she finished wrapping his arm in the clean bandage. His voice raspy, he said, "I could use some water, please, miss?"

She found a canteen nearby, and eased it to his mouth. He swallowed once, then twice, then gave a nod. He smiled again as she eased his head down.

"It's a great battle on that little round hilltop. You are brave to come into this place, much braver than I. I could never walk into such a valley of death. I wouldn't even consider it, except . . ." The soldier glanced at his wounds and smiled.

The smile seemed to carry the sun in it. And Tillie felt her breathing ease; even her trembling seemed to stop.

"You must excuse my boldness, miss. But I think it rude of me to continue calling on you without knowing your name."

"Tillie." She cleared her throat. "My name is Tillie."

"And I am Warrick, and much pleased to make your acquaintance." He coughed. How odd to smile in such a wretched place. It was like a blanket, wrapping her in warmth on a cold winter night. He had blue eyes the color of sky, and even in the gloom they shone with sunshine. She offered him another drink. "I could do with a favor, Miss Tillie.

I've not had time to write my mama. I've been thinking I should write to her, to tell her I'm all right."

"I will write your letter, sir," Tillie said. "I'll need to find a pen and paper."

She dashed off, glad for her new chore, away from the pools of blood, flies, and maggots. She had always done well in school. There was no agony in writing letters, no pain, no screaming. She returned from the house not long after, carrying all that she needed for letter-writing. Carefully she laid them before her. The soldier—Warrick—watched her, smiling the while.

"Miss Tillie, your kindness is god-sent," Warrick said. "But you needn't call me sir. I'm no officer, and I'm certainly not my father. Please call me Warrick?"

She poised her pen, dipping the tip in ink. "Well, then, Warrick, you tell me what you want to say. Then I will read it back to you, to make sure it's perfect."

"Dear Mama," Warrick began.

And Tillie wrote, careful to write each letter perfectly. Sometimes Warrick stammered, not sure of what to say.

"You are doing your mother proud," Tillie reassured him.

"I cannot think of the right word, one pleasing enough for my mama," he said.

"Tell me what you miss about your home."

Warrick thought a moment, and his smile brightened. "It's the strangest thing, how memory can play the cleverest tricks on a mind. While I was home, I thought there could be no smaller place than that. And now, when I look back, I think not all of heaven could be so grand as that small house near the sea. I miss that salty air that fills a body up. I miss Mama, smelling like her peach pie. And Papa smelled like a good pipe at the end of a long day. I miss my little sister, Becca. She has a smell all her own, clean and new like spring rain."

"Seems to me, perhaps you should say exactly that," said Tillie. How odd that only the week before, she had dreamed of adventure, of leaving Gettysburg, and now all she wanted to do was go home. Wasn't that what that runaway said, too? She just wanted to go home?

The minutes slipped into an hour, and he finished telling his letter.

"Your loving and devoted son, Warrick," she finished reading.

"Why, you paint some picture of me!" Warrick chuckled. "Your letter makes me sound better than I am."

"Your mama will be very proud of you," Tillie said. "And she will tell you as much when you get home. Right now, perhaps you need sleep."

"I am a bit tired. And if I may be so bold, again, might I ask you come by again, Miss Tillie?"

"You are indeed too bold, Warrick." She smiled, an easy smile one shares with an old friend.

"Then consider yourself asked!" He chuckled, then coughed.

"And I promise I will surely do that!" Tillie smiled. And he fell asleep.

She felt she could breathe again, and could do something to help. Tillie moved among the wounded, offering water and writing letters. Sometimes all they wanted to do was talk. And so she listened. The acrid smells of blood and death seemed to soften. Even the moans seemed less. Once in a while she looked back at Warrick, still in peaceful sleep.

Then, sometime in the late afternoon, the dark-haired nurse approached her.

"Perhaps you should take a rest yourself, miss. You've been here almost as long as I have been, which is far too long."

"I'm quite fine, sir." Tillie smiled.

"Did I say that you are an angel, miss? And a right fine nurse."

Tillie shook her head. "I've not done much of anything but write letters."

"You're an angel, and let no one tell you otherwise. You've lasted longer than the others." The nurse chuckled. "It's not an easy thing, to be amid such death. You showed uncommon kindness, and certainly to that one, a rebel at that. Not too many could do that."

"Rebel?" Tillie stiffened. *Rebel?*

The nurse nodded toward Warrick. "When men are wounded, no

matter the age or cause that moves them, they all become like sons in need of a mother's comfort."

Tillie's heart quivered. He was not like anything she had expected. He didn't wear a uniform, or talk like one of them! She walked toward the sleeping soldier. What could she say to him? He had been kind, and had eased her own trembling. She wanted to say something. She wanted to say—thank you.

Still he slept. She walked softer so as not to wake him. As she came closer, however, she realized he wasn't asleep.

He had died. Warrick had died.

He only wanted to go home, to see his mama. Just like Grace, and the dark-eyed runaway.

Just like her.

Once again she began to tremble, and this time she thought it would never stop.

CHAPTER TWENTY-FOUR

GRACE

Boom! Boom! Boom!

She thought the roar of the cannons would never end. Grace lay there, her face buried in the dirt of the root cellar's floor. Her hands were pressed tight against her ears, trying to dull the noise. But each time she hoped to breathe, *Boom! Boom! Boom!* Her very bones quivered.

Wisdom huddled with her sister, eyes clenched as tight as their arms about each other.

Boom! Boom! Boom! Hour after hour. The dark pressed in all around.

Mrs. Woods never came.

Friend Alice never came.

Pappa never came.

Boom! Boom! Boom!

PART TWELVE

THE
THIRD
DAY

Friday, July 3

CHAPTER TWENTY-FIVE

ANNIE

Her feet were on fire.

The day before, they had marched thirty miles, leaving Chambersburg before the sun rose and reaching Cashtown Gap with the sun beating down sure as any determined drummer. When the column finally reached the tiny town of Cashtown, soldiers sprawled on the ground, too weary even to eat. Everyone listened for battle news. Annie and Dylan found the wagons. Jasper sat there in wait for them.

"Jiggers." He forced a smile. "At least I got here in one piece, more or less."

As the battle raged in the town of Gettysburg, three miles away, the three shared a fire and listened. *Boom! Boom! Boom!*

When the sun rose, that was where they were going.

Dylan's growl was gone, his crooked grin was straightened, his eyes were dulled with uncommon worry. He spat into the fire, then spoke in a low voice, handing Annie a tintype.

"I wish you to take my likeness and send it to my mother with a letter."

Annie took the picture and tucked it into her inside pocket.

Gideon gave his son a nod, puffing circles with his pipe. Then, looking to her, he said, "You spent, son?"

"I'm tolerable," she said.

Gideon smiled. "You wrote to your mama, son?"

Annie shook her head. "Mama wouldn't approve of me going into the army. She has certain ideas how things ought to be. She can be mighty stubborn sometimes."

Gideon tapped his pipe carefully. "Nothing worse than a stubborn woman, I suppose."

Annie grinned. "Mama's pretty tough."

Gideon tapped his pipe harder, dumping the burned tobacco, the last of Mrs. Trudeau's treasures. He pointed to Dylan. "Dylan, he's a good boy, but he carries a good-size chip on his shoulder . . ."

"Aww, Pop." Dylan rolled his eyes, then rolled up in his blanket.

". . . and he sniffs out trouble better than a bloodhound." Gideon chuckled. "He's got a wild streak that's made for some worrisome moments. Tried everything I could to tame that streak of lightning, but can't tame an elemental. His mama used to coddle that boy. I told her once, it'll be the ruin him. His mama tells me, 'He's just like you, old man, always at the front of things.' I saw it for what it was; I was just afeared for him, not wanting him to see the hardness of life. Parents can get mighty stubborn about fearing for their babies."

"So," Annie whispered, nodding in understanding, "I should write my mama."

"Can't tell you what to do, son." Gideon packed his pipe away. "You're a man now, and a man's responsible for his decisions."

Annie listened to the battle noises. Even after the booming finally quieted, she listened as everyone around her talked on, smoked their last pipes, wrote their last letters, waiting in the dark for the moment when it was their turn to face the elephant.

It was the clearest of nights, the moon bright and bold. And there the North Star shone true. In that moment, she understood. And the world seemed a terrible good place to be. It wasn't patriotism that sent her here. It wasn't to avenge her brothers. She had no thoughts about slaves, but she understood their need to be free, their need to control their own destiny, to be who they are.

She finally saw her place in it all. Before her stretched all the possibility she could imagine. Because Pap made her stubborn and Mama made her tough. And because William made her dream big. She *could* find her own place, way out west, and make it what she wanted it to be.

At last she breathed as easy as she ever did, long ago at home.

The moment came.

Three in the morning, the drum rolled. Annie blinked. It hurt to pull her boots on.

The drum rolled again.

Dylan was already awake. He gave a stout nod. *So it begins.*

As they waited for the final word to march, Gideon brewed potato coffee. Annie had near forgot what true coffee tasted like.

For that matter, she had forgot what true food tasted like.

And the word came: "Fall in!" Gideon called out. "Boys of Virginia, your time awaits!"

CHAPTER TWENTY-SIX

Dawn broke still as pond water, and the army was already on the march, moving east along the Pike. As the bloody sun broke free of the horizon, the mist rose, too. The air heated steadily, another hellfire day.

The column turned onto a rutted farm trail, moving south of town. Everywhere the road and the fields were littered with the wrecked bodies of the dead, the mangled bodies of the dying. No one said a word, taking their hats off in respect.

Annie kept her eyes on the boots ahead of her.

Then the column turned east, and the road narrowed even more. They marched past a large farm and soon found themselves snaking along a ridge that stretched for miles. Seminary Ridge. Finally the massive column came to a halt. The Ninth Virginia had reached the southernmost end of the ridge, marked by orchards grown wild, when Gideon called out: "At ease!"

Annie flopped on the ground as others spread out to find water.

"Went to look for my own self what we're facing," said one soldier. "We're about to reap the whirlwind, chums. Across the way is Cemetery Ridge, where the Federals have the higher ground and the tighter formation. We're stretched from here to eternity. Wouldn't give a plugged nickel for my life's worth about now."

"As I see it," Dylan said from where he lay, "this division was selected because we are Virginians. Because we succeed where others fail."

"Pickett's too busy looking dandy to see what's going on," Gideon said.

Annie had seen General Pickett ride up and down the lines. He had long ringlets that flowed to his shoulders, a drooping mustache and a goatee, and he dressed too much like a dandy to inspire ordinary men into battle.

Annie, with the rest of the Ninth Virginia, took position in a hollow surrounded by apple trees. They were fine old trees, holding apples that were green and small, and no doubt too sour for anything but throwing.

Dylan plucked a few of the green apples and pelted others down the line. He hooted as he hit his mark. He never missed. Well, almost never. Soon enough, the others were returning fire. Annie ducked as an apple struck her leg.

For a moment they laughed.

"Heads up, strawfoot," Dylan called out just as another apple hit her haversack.

She looked to the branches overhead, how the sun dappled the leaves. No tree grew as tall as that old live oak in her field at home. Now it seemed even taller in her memory. And there in her memory, in the topmost branches of that old oak, sat William, all a-smile.

He seemed to whisper, *You've done right by yourself.*

The air crackled with musket fire along the ridge.

"Stay calm, boys." Gideon spoke in an even tone. He walked up and down behind the line. "Keep steady. No shouting, no shooting. Let's not tell them where we are."

But despite the orders, shouts rumbled at the other end of the infantry line. There General Pickett rode, his horse trotting next to General Longstreet's. There were others riding along, too. But then she saw a great white horse, as great a horse as Pap's colt had been, the colt he had traded for her Whitworth. Atop the horse was a fine old gentleman. The rider was not as tall as she'd imagined, but certainly he was dignified, dressed in a well-worn long gray jacket, high black felt hat, and blue trousers tucked into his boots. She knew him, sure enough.

General Robert E. Lee.

And the men cheered as he rode by.

The other horsemen accompanying him rode up and down, speaking with the officers of the line. Soon enough, the riders approached Major Owens, who then called Sergeant Gideon over. Their heads huddled close for a long while.

Annie drank heavily from her canteen. How could a day get so hot?

Gideon returned, calling the boys over.

"Dig in, sons," he said. "It'll be a while yet. But soon, soon. And when the orders come, we'll be taking that ridge." He pointed across the field of tall grass stretching out before them, to a clump of trees that broke the horizon.

Dylan whistled. He brushed his red hair aside, more in amazement than from sweat.

"That's over a mile away! We'll be walking through hell before we get to that ridge!"

Gideon nodded. "Boys, I'll not be lying to you. Some hundred yards out, we'll be heading into the range of the sharpshooters. But you hold steady to that clump. Your friends will fall, but I tell you, keep steady. Even as the enemy shower us with their cannon! Keep steady. You'll lose friends, but we'll take that hill! For Virginia, boys!"

The men whooped. Gideon gave Dylan a shake. He kept hold of his son's hand a while longer, and Annie knew that in his own way, he was saying good-bye. Then the sergeant turned and slapped Annie on the shoulder. The minutes rolled into hours. *Hurry up and wait.*

For a time it seemed the world stopped, the war stopped. Annie looked up, saw the blue sky, and imagined where William's star might be flying about now. When she got out, yesirree, she'd go west, get her own land, and she'd plant an oak, a mighty oak, on top of a hill, let it grow as old as time, so she could see the North Star. . . .

Then it began.

First one, then the next, the cannons opened fire down the line, the world exploding in plumes of white smoke. The billows drifted across the field, thick as fog.

"Steady, sons," Gideon reassured them.

Boom! Boom! Boom!

The Federals returned fire. The air was alive with screaming shells and flying fragments.

Annie dug even lower to the ground as a fragment whistled above her head. Someone gasped behind her. She chanced a quick look back over her shoulder, and saw that a soldier had caught the fragment square. But she couldn't tell who it was. He didn't have a face.

"Hold steady, boys!" Gideon shouted.

Boom! Boom! Boom!

For an hour it rained fire. More boys fell to the flying fragments.

And then the cannons stopped. It was a mean silence, as thundering as the cannon fire.

"Fall in!" Gideon stood tall. "It's time, sons! This is the moment that'll define your life, heroes of Virginia! For your mother, then, and for your sisters! Stand tall, boys. Stand tall as you might!"

And the boys of the Ninth Regiment stood tall as they might. There were none taller.

Annie looked up Seminary Ridge. Stretched along the rise for over a mile, twelve thousand men stood tall as they might.

These were the boys of Virginia, all around her. Farther down the line stood the boys of North Carolina, South Carolina, Georgia, and Louisiana. There were so many, and James Anachie Gordon had lived among them, had earned his measure as one of them.

"Strawfoot," Dylan said, standing next to her, "it might be that I am a coward by nature, as big as any might be. But if all my friends march forward, I'll march beside them—with great pride." He looked squarely at Annie. He looked so hard that, for a moment, she thought he'd discovered her secret.

"You've been a pain in my backside from the very beginning," Annie said. "And I'm quite proud to march beside you."

Below the lines, General Pickett rode up and down his division. His curls were flying. His horse was prancing. He waved his sword above his head.

"Look to the heights to take, heroes of Virginia!" he shouted. "See the greatness of the moment. Remember, today we are all Virginians!"

"Portsmouth Rifles, up and at 'em!" Gideon shouted. "*Destiny awaits!*"

The first cannon rang out. The men moved into formation, a wall of men stretching more than a mile down the ridge.

The second shot rang out.

"Right shoulder, shift arms! Forward, march!" The order echoed down the line.

Bayonets glistening in the hot sun, the wall of men stepped off the rise in perfect order. The cannoneers cheered as the soldiers moved through the artillery line, into the open fields.

The line had advanced less than two hundred yards when the Federals sent shell after shell howling into their midst.

Boom! Boom! Boom!

The shells exploded, leaving holes where the earth had been. Shells pummeled the marching men. As one man fell in the front of the line, another stepped up to take his place. Smoke billowed into a curtain of white, thick and heavy as fog, stalking them across the field.

Still they marched on. They held their fire, waiting for the order.

Boom! A riderless horse, wide-eyed and bloodied, emerged from the cloud of smoke. It screamed in panic as another shell exploded.

Boom! All around lay the dead and dying. There seemed more dead than living now. Men fell legless, headless, armless, black with burns and red with blood.

Boom! The very earth shook with the terrible hellfire.

Still they marched on.

A high whine zipped close to her as the Yankee sharpshooters opened fire.

Keep steady, boys!

For more than a mile they marched, ninety steps a minute.

Annie leaned forward, holding her hat down as if hit by a hailstorm. But all around, soldiers fell like stalks of corn as bullets found their mark.

Jasper spun hard about, falling like the others as a bullet hit true.

Keep steady, boys! Do not hurry or fire too fast! Wait until I give the order!

Ahead was nothing but smoke and flames. As they neared the

road, they came to a rail fence that divided the fields. The fence slowed them down, but it couldn't stop them. They climbed over the fence, some picked off like ducks on a farm by the blue-belly fire. But still they marched on and crossed the road.

Then the rebel wall of men raised such a thundering holler, the very heart of every man stirred anew.

Annie yodeled as loud as anyone, raising her Whitworth in defiance.

And Dylan yodeled, his crooked grin wide. And they marched on, the trees not eight hundred yards away. Federals poured down from the right and the left, meeting at a stone wall.

"Now, boys! Gideon shouted. And the order came. "Now, sons of Virginia! Fire!"

Annie fired, rushing forward.

PART THIRTEEN

THE DAY AFTER

Sunday, July 4

CHAPTER TWENTY-SEVEN

The moon rode high, and the stars were bright, but already clouds were moving in. By morning light, the drizzle began. Then thunderstorms rumbled over the little town. The rain filled the creeks to overflowing, but it did little to wash away the blood.

The Confederate army was leaving. General Lee led the way back to Virginia. Behind him came the wagons carrying the wounded, trailing for seventeen miles.

Left behind in the homes of Gettysburg, and in the fields and rocky hills and ridges surrounding the small town, were thousands more men—the dying who had no hope of surviving, and the dead.

The Battle of Gettysburg was done.

PART FOURTEEN

THE DAYS
AFTER
THE BATTLE

CHAPTER TWENTY-EIGHT

GRACE

The quiet proved more deafening than the cannon fire, and it scared Grace to the bone. They dared not move from the cellar. Off and on they heard frantic shouting, shooting, and stomping. But who was shouting? Who was shooting? And whom were they shooting?

Mrs. Woods never came.

Mr. Butler never came.

They were forgotten, there in the darkness.

"Does she ever talk?" Grace asked Wisdom, pointing to Sorry. Sorry crouched near a crate, close to the light. They were running out of candles.

"Not unless she has something to say, which is none too often."

"Is that why you call her Sorry?"

"I don't call her Sorry," Wisdom said. "That's what *they* call her."

"What do you call her?"

"That's not my name to give. But the story is something else. Once long ago in a faraway land lived a king who lost his queen. Out of loneliness, this king sent his messengers throughout the lands to find him a new queen. It weren't too long before they came upon a particularly beautiful woman named Esther."

Grace smiled. Wisdom's voice was like the mourning doves that called to the sun.

"When the king saw her, he fell madly in love with her. Unknown to the king, however, Esther was Jewish. And her father was Mordecai, who refused to bow to the king. He felt no man should bow before another. This made the king very angry, and he made a law to put all Jews to death. When Esther found out, she went to her king. Even though she knew it might mean her death. She became the voice that saved them."

"Your sister's name is Esther." Grace smiled as Wisdom nodded, the two looking to Sorry—Esther—who frowned.

A chill seeped into the little hole, and Grace knew it had begun to rain. Water began to seep down the outside wall. It seeped across the dirt floor, turning it to mud.

And more rain came, and now Grace feared the cellar was flooding.

"We cannot stay here," Grace announced.

"We don't know who's up there," said Wisdom.

"But we know what's down here," Grace said. "We *can't* stay."

Unable to sit up, Grace pushed against the shutter. She slipped in the mud, and lost her hold. The shutter didn't move. The cellar had flooded, and the water had moved something in front of the panel.

The water now rushed down the wall. The mud deepened and the water began to pool around them.

Esther eased next to Grace, and both pushed against the shutter, both sliding in the mud. The water was now pooled so deep that it ran across the floor, snaking its way to the shutter and under the wood. It rushed like a river, and it was getting deeper.

"We need to get a firmer foothold," said Grace. Wisdom braced her feet against the wall, and Grace, her feet on Wisdom's shoulders, pushed against the panel. Wisdom groaned with the force, but it didn't move. Now Grace and Esther braced their feet against Wisdom's shoulders, their hands firmly planted on the shutter. Together they lunged forward with their full strength. The shutter shivered, but did not move.

At that moment, water-soaked dirt fell in chunks from the wall. Wisdom squealed. Esther inhaled sharply. Grace realized with horror that the walls were crumbling around them. They were going to be buried alive!

"Again!" Grace shouted.

Grace and Esther heaved, both yelling as they did so. Grace pushed so hard that she thought her arms would snap in two.

"Again!"

The shutter shivered, then at last it moved. Another kick, and finally it fell away. And the two tumbled over the drop, plunging into a cold, wet pool. The cellar had flooded level with the floor of the little room, and the water was still rising. Something smashed into the side of Grace's head, and she reeled from the pain.

And that same moment the hiding place collapsed, creating a surge of water that tossed Grace backward. She struggled to gather her feet, slipping on the muddy floor. The water was now to her waist and still rising fast. The slash across her head throbbed so that she heard nothing but ringing in her ears.

And then she saw that Esther was screaming, screaming and clawing at the wall where the room had been, where Wisdom still lay inside.

Grace screamed, too, such screaming as to chase away the ringing in her head and the noise of the water rushing around them. Such screaming as overtakes everything and everyone. She clawed into the wall where the room had been, where Wisdom still lay. She screamed until her throat burned raw.

She didn't hear the stomping above her. But she saw the shadows of three figures bound down the stairs. She saw Mr. Butler rush to the back wall, throwing his full strength into digging through the mud.

She saw Mrs. Woods hold Esther close to her, patting her shoulders in comfort, as the two cried as hard as the rain.

And she saw Pappa lift her in his arms. She wrapped her arms about his neck so tight, she thought she would never let go.

And still she screamed, until she lost her voice. And then she sobbed, so hard as to rock her still.

CHAPTER TWENTY-NINE

Wade in the water, wade in the water, children. . . .

Grace woke to the sounds of the singing. It wrapped about her like a warm quilt. Her head throbbed. The air was so heavy with stench that it hurt to breathe.

"Wade in the water, God's gonna trouble the water."

Grace smiled up at Esther. Esther sang, her voice as sad as moonlight, and yet it shone as bright.

"I'm sorry," Grace whispered. Her throat burned raw. The words seemed too small for what she felt.

"You've not anything to feel sorry for," Esther said. Her eyes were red, but she wasn't crying anymore. In fact, she was smiling down at Grace. "I remember Mam, and this she said to me: 'Sorrow holds the hand of joy in this dance of life.' You've done nothing, Grace, but treat us like kin. Friend Alice is here. She's taking me up north straightway. Seems like some folk want to hear my story. But I wasn't going anywhere until you woke up, not until I could tell you: Thank you, Grace Bryan."

Esther bent low to hug Grace.

"Thank you, Grace Bryan," she whispered.

"Hey there, baby girl." Pappa walked into the room.

Even though it hurt to move, Grace bounded from the bed, and Papa scooped her into his arms.

"Girl, don't you ever stay put?" He laughed.

"Good thing you didn't stay with Miss Mary." Friend Alice walked in behind Pappa. "The Confederates took over her home just hours after you left. You would have been caught for sure, then there's no telling what might have happened."

"Friend Alice." Grace smiled. "You're all right."

"These are terrible days," Friend Alice said. "Try as I might, I couldn't get back. I heard rebels had taken some poor people not far from here and hung the family that kept them. The friends that kept me wouldn't allow me to venture out until the rebels left. Now people from all around are swarming into Gettysburg to help with the wounded, in hopes of finding their own lost loves. The roadways are clogged with the traffic. All that rain didn't help matters. The fever has broken out in some of the hospitals. I fear Gettysburg is in for a few more rough weeks. Esther and I need to move quickly."

Friend Alice hugged Grace and shook Pappa's hand. Grace clasped Esther's hand. It was hard to let go.

"We have our own travels ahead," Pappa said then, easing her back onto the bed. "Mr. Butler is heading for Philadelphia, taking us to your mamma. You up to that?"

"I can do anything, Pappa," Grace said. *Except face Mamma*, she thought, her foot tap-tap-tapping. "We're coming back, Pappa?"

"Gettysburg is our home. There's much work to be done, and we can do it."

"Yes, we can," Grace whispered, and she smiled.

CHAPTER THIRTY

TILLIE

Tillie and Henrietta made their way slowly up Taneytown Road. They were singing, but it was more like a prayer at the Sunday service. *Weeping, sad and lonely, hopes and fears how vain! When this cruel war is over, praying that we meet again.*

No one had dared leave the farm for days after the battle. Tillie thought of Warrick, and felt her pocket to make sure his letter was safe. She meant to send it home as soon as she could, like she'd promised. Tillie shook her head, her heart hurting more than any scolding from Mother could.

The air was thick with the smell of death and dying, stinging her eyes like a thousand bees. Tillie pulled her scarf about her face and breathed shallow, gritting her teeth against the smell. The wounded still groaned, and shrieked, and sobbed piteously, lying next to the bodies of their dead comrades now bloating in the heat. There was such despair all around, on this field of blood. Ambulances drove from the fields to the hospitals—hospitals set up in every home, church, and barn of Gettysburg—while nurses and surgeons, sisters from the church, and families searched the fields for the living. Soldiers, too, searched for their comrades.

The roads were crowded again with families from near and far coming in hopes of finding their loved ones. Men and women from charities had come to lend their help. Newspaper reporters scurried about, looking for stories.

To the west, across the road and field to Seminary Ridge, Tillie saw the dead and dying lying everywhere. Thousands of them. Union soldiers, serving as grave diggers, piled as many bodies as could fit in shallow graves. But there were not enough men to bury the dead. Clouds of flies feasted on the living as well as the dead. And if there were not enough men to bury their dead, there were none to bury the horses, their bloated bodies grotesque in the sun.

It was all Tillie could do to stand. She had to sit for a moment, so she stumbled to a stone wall where she eased forward, holding her stomach and her head.

"It was the grandest sight I ever saw," she heard someone say. She looked up to see a soldier sitting in the shadows against a tree trunk not far from her. The soldier cradled a rifle in both arms, and seemed all aquiver. He wasn't speaking to anyone, just talking to himself.

"They kept coming." He shook his head in disbelief. "We threw everything at 'em, and they still kept coming. They charged with that yell of theirs, sounding as if all of hell was in that cry. I ain't never heard such a thing as that rebel yell. For as long as I live, I'll hear that yell. They kept coming, knowing full well they were marching to their death. Such a sight as that, right out of the schoolbooks. We saw history here."

Tillie stooped near him and touched his hand. "Sir, it's been done for days. How long have you been here?"

"Since the first shot, to the last. A lifetime in between, miss."

"Come with us. We'll see you safe."

The soldier shook his head. "I'm fine, miss. Just need to sit a bit more."

"Do you need anything, sir?" said Tillie.

The soldier looked up at her. Suddenly there was a great worry in his eyes; his brow twisted in concern. "Found this here rifle over by that tree, where the stone walls meet. This here is a mighty fine rifle, a Whitworth. I took it off a Confederate fallen. Do you think he'd mind if I took it? Not to shoot it, no, no. I'll hang it in a place of honor. And I'll tell everyone what I saw here. That kind of courage deserves to be remembered."

"I think he'd appreciate it greatly, sir."

The soldier smiled, relieved. He said, "I found these with him."

The soldier held out a bundle of letters. There was a tintype of a lanky soldier with a crooked grin. It was blurred somewhat, but that crooked grin showed clearly. There were letters, too. "I don't know what to do with these. But I couldn't just leave them."

"I'll take these letters," Tillie said. "I promise you, I will see to it that they get home. I think you should go home, sir. And don't you worry none. I will do right by our soldiers."

The soldier pointed to where a copse of trees came together with a stone wall, where lay a mangled heap of fallen soldiers, both Union and Confederate.

Stepping lightly over the corpses, she had to lean in close to see their faces. Sometimes she had to move aside caps, hands, and torn linen, searching the broken and bloodied remains.

She roamed the fallen, waving aside the flies as she picked through their pockets and knapsacks. Every letter she found, every picture, she would send home. She meant to send them all home, no matter how long it took.

Henrietta and the other women saw what Tillie was doing. They nodded to each other and began to help. Tillie plucked the letters and the pictures and wrapped them carefully. She took a knapsack and filled it. Then she found another knapsack and filled that one, too.

She was going to make sure their loved ones knew where their sons and husbands and brothers had fallen. They were all somebody's son, or husband, or brother, or friend.

They all deserved to go home.

She carried all she could carry, satchels and pouches stuffed with letters and photographs. She looked out across the field, all the way to the ridge, and behind her. She stiffened. There were so many left. . . .

"I'll come back," she promised.

Somewhere ahead on the road, someone laughed, a booming laugh. She searched the sea of soldiers and townsfolk. It didn't take long to find the laughter. No one could miss Abraham Bryan.

And there beside him . . .

"Grace!" Tillie shouted, waving her hand. "Grace Bryan!"

Grace Bryan had made it after all! And the runaways—did they find their way to freedom?

Weaving through the crowd, she caught Grace and her pappa standing amid the trampled mess of their garden and orchard. Next to them stood Mr. Butler.

Her heart was near bursting to see Grace standing there. And all the moments of the last few days started to well up.

"I'm sorry what happened to your home," she said. She wanted to say more.

Grace shuffled her feet and cleared her throat. She seemed small and confused.

"How's your cheek?" Grace said.

Tillie touched her cheek and smiled. "Mother said I should be careful when picking flowers in the middle of the night."

Now Grace smiled.

Tillie cleared her throat. "I've been wanting to know . . . I've been thinking about your *sisters*, and hoping they made it safely home. I surely hope they did, you know."

Grace shook her head, tears welling. She swallowed hard, and it took a long moment for her to speak. "Esther says hey."

And Tillie, understanding, felt her own tears well.

"I'm very sorry," she whispered. She looked across the tortured ruins of the peach orchard. "They were the best peaches, so full of sunshine and sweetness. I took some for my mother, so you know. She was feeling the weight of the world, and I thought, if she could just eat one of those peaches, it would make everything better."

"And did it?" Grace asked.

"For a little while." Tillie nodded, but her own tears flowed freely. She wiped them away.

"There'll be more peaches again someday. You wait." Grace smiled. "Then you can *take* more peaches. But I'll chase you down, just so you know. I have little tolerance for thieves."

"I'll be sure to give you fair warning, to give you a head start," Tillie said. "I promise."

Mr. Butler said then, "Heard tell about some peaches once that grew so large, a farmer had to use a wheelbarrow to harvest one peach at a time."

"That true?" Abraham Bryan smiled.

"True enough," Mr. Butler said.

And Tillie smiled, too, glad to be home.

CHAPTER THIRTY-ONE

ANNIE

Dear Mama,

I hope this letter finds you feeling better. I know I have disappointed you. Forgive me. I am well, Mama, so do not worry. I have traveled through many towns, and have seen some handsome country. Such terrible wonders I have seen.

I'm thinking to go west once I am done. I would have my own land. William said I can do anything I set my mind to, and seems to me I can't live a better life than that.

We will be marching soon. I do not know how long before I have to go onto the field of battle.

Dear Mama, I am not afraid, so you be not afraid. There is not a Yank bullet made for me yet! But if it is God's will, so be it. And I will wait for you in heaven, then, with a warm embrace. I will be there with William and with James. Pap will be smiling again, waiting for you. It will be a happy time. Until then, Mama, you should look north to William's star. I'll be looking, too. We'll all be looking. There's a comfort in that knowing.

> I think of you every day.
> Your devoted A.

Thursday, November 19, 1863

President Abraham Lincoln was nervous. The famous orator Edward Everett, the featured speaker of the day, had held the audience spellbound for two hours, moving them to tears. Lincoln also felt weak from fever, and his head ached. He worried for his son, Tad, who had fallen ill. His wife, Mary, had begged him not to go. His personal secretary, John Hay, noted that Lincoln's face had a ghastly color and his expression was haggard.

But the president was determined to speak at the ceremony for the new national cemetery at Gettysburg, to honor the soldiers who had died in the battle there. The field where Pickett made his charge still showed the ravages of war. The town, too, still bore the signs that a great battle had moved through its streets.

President Lincoln stepped slowly to the platform, and standing before twenty thousand spectators, his hands clasped in front of him, he spoke:

Four score and seven years ago our fathers brought forth on this continent, a new nation, conceived in liberty, and dedicated to the proposition that all men are created equal.

Now we are engaged in a great civil war, testing whether that nation, or any nation so conceived and so dedicated, can long endure. We are met on a great battlefield of that war. We have come to dedicate a portion of that field, as a final resting place for those who here gave their lives that that nation might live. It is altogether fitting and proper that we should do this.

But, in a larger sense, we cannot dedicate—we cannot consecrate—we cannot hallow—this ground. The brave men, living and dead, who struggled here, have consecrated it, far above our poor power to add or detract. The world will little note, nor long remember what we say here, but it can never forget what they did here. It is for us the living, rather, to be dedicated here to the unfinished work which they who fought here have thus far so nobly advanced. It is rather for us to be here dedicated to the great task remaining before us—that from these honored dead we take increased devotion to that cause for which they gave the last full measure of devotion— that we here highly resolve that these dead shall not have died in vain—that this nation, under God, shall have a new birth of freedom—and that government of the people, by the people, for the people, shall not perish from the earth.

At the end of his "little speech," as he later called it, the audience erupted in applause. Everett was so moved that he thanked the president for the "eloquent simplicity and appropriateness" of his remarks, adding, "I should be glad, if I could flatter myself that I came as near to the central idea of the occasion, in two hours, as you did in two minutes."

Lincoln replied, "I am pleased to know that, in your judgment, the little I did say was not entirely a failure."

AUTHOR'S NOTE

Between five hundred and one thousand women disguised themselves as men and enlisted in the Union and Confederate armies. Only the letters written by three women soldiers have been found. Diaries, if any existed, have not survived. Only two women soldiers, Sarah Edmonds and Loretta Janeta Velazquez, published their memoirs after the war.

Tillie Pierce was fifteen at the time of the battle. Her diary, *At Gettysburg: Or, What a Girl Saw and Heard of the Battle*, was published in 1889.

Miss Mary McAllister was a 41-year-old spinster and store owner when the Confederate and Union forces marched through Gettysburg. Her family was very active in the Underground Railroad. Visitors can still see the houses, caves, and other sites that were used as safe houses and hideaways. Two interesting books that explore the experiences of the women in Gettysburg are E. F. Conklin's *Women in Gettysburg: 1863* (Gettysburg, PA: Thomas Publications, 1993) and William G. Williams's *Days of Darkness: The Gettysburg Civilians* (Shippensburg, PA: White Mane Publishing, 1986).

Abraham Bryan owned twelve acres south of Gettysburg, complete with two houses and a barn. As a landowner, he was one of the economic elite of the town. Unable to read and write, he left no personal recording about his life seven miles north of the Mason-Dixon Line nor about his observations of the battle. What little information is known comes from tax and census records and from legal documents that he filed because of damages to his farm.

Before the Civil War, the African-American community in Gettysburg flourished. Of the 2,500 citizens of Gettysburg, more than 250 were African-American. Many of the black citizens were involved in the Underground Railroad. In 1834 a school was established for the children of African Americans. In 1839 the school was moved to St. Paul's Church. The curriculum focused on reading and math skills, considered essential in achieving economic success. During the war, most of the community fled north, never to return. Seven years after the war, nearly two-thirds of the African-American community lived elsewhere.

However, Abraham Bryan did return to Gettysburg with his family. He rebuilt his farm, which had been destroyed during the battle. In 1869 he sold his farm and moved into town, where he lived comfortably, managing the local hotel until his death in 1879. For more information on the African-American community at the time of the Battle of Gettysburg, read Peter C. Vermilyea's "The Effect of the Confederate Invasion of Pennsylvania on Gettysburg's African American Community" in *Gettysburg Magazine* at www.gdg.org/gettysburg%20 magazine/gburgafrican.html.

To re-create the story of Annie, Grace, and Tillie, I drew upon diaries and many other documents, including town records, regimental records, government documents, and current research on the battle. Scott Hartwig, supervisory historian of Gettysburg National Military Park, and the National Park Service provided invaluable help. So, too, did the wonderful people at the park bookstore. Re-enactors and historians Dave Pueschel and Mark Strojek were wonderfully generous with their information on the life of a Confederate soldier in the Ninth Virginia Infantry Regiment. Among the most valuable readings, but certainly not the whole of the list, are John Dooley, *Confederate Soldier: His War Journal* (Washington, D.C.: Georgetown University Press, 1945); Thomas Francis Galway's journal in *The Valiant Hours* (Mechanicsburg, PA: Stackpole Books, 1946); Mark Nesbitt's *35 Days to Gettysburg: The Campaign Diaries of Two Enemies* (Mechanicsburg, PA: Stackpole Books, 1992); Albert Nofi's detailed analysis of the battle, including personalities, strategy, geographical studies, and even weather patterns, in *The Gettysburg Campaign* (Conshohocken, PA: Combined Books, 1986); the invaluable *Pickett's Charge: Eyewitness Accounts*, edited by Richard Rollins (Redondo Beach, CA: Rank and File Publications, 1994); and Benjamin Trask's definitive regimental history, *9th Virginia Infantry* (Lynchburg, VA: H. E. Howard, 1984).

An estimated 618,000 to 700,000 Americans, both civilians and soldiers, lost their lives during the Civil War, more than in the

Revolutionary War, the War of 1812, the Mexican War, the Spanish-American War, the two World Wars, and the Korean War combined. This was the time before dog tags or other means of identification, and close to half who died remained "unknown soldiers." Neither the North nor the South kept accurate records of its causalities. Families often never learned the fate of their sons, husbands, and brothers.

On November 19, 1863, the town of Gettysburg opened a new cemetery to honor the fallen. Although feeling sick on that day, President Lincoln delivered his "Gettysburg Address" at the opening ceremony for the new cemetery. He was later diagnosed with a mild case of smallpox. For an eyewitness account of the events of that day, see Tyler Dennett's *Lincoln and the Civil War in the Diaries and Letters of John Hay* (New York: Dodd, Mead & Co., 1939); Phillip B. Kunhardt's *A New Birth of Freedom: Lincoln at Gettysburg* (New York: Little, Brown & Co., 1983); and Carl Sandburg's *Abraham Lincoln: The War Years* (New York: Harcourt, Brace & Co., 1939). Edward Everett's November 20, 1863, letter to Abraham Lincoln is in the collection of the Library of Congress and can be seen at www.loc.gov/exhibits/treasures/trt032.html.

My special thanks to Julie Amper, most fabulous editor, for going on this journey with me, and to Harold Underdown, for his insights while I was his student during his Kid's Book Revisions workshops.

While I did my best to stay true to the times and the people, I did imagine discussions and make leaps of logic for the sake of character and plot. In the end, I am just a storyteller, not a historian.

But then again, all of history is a story.